THE TROUBLE WITH AN EVERLASTING COWBOY

Texas Matchmakers At It Again, Book Two

DEBRA CLOPTON

The Trouble with an Everlasting Cowboy

Welcome back to Mule Hollow for a romance that's sure to make you smile. No, it's not *Bad, Bad Leroy Brown,* but like the old song there's trouble brewing and romance that won't go away…

Max Cantrell is building his Mule Hollow Prickly Pear Jelly Company business that he and his mom opened a few years after they came to Mule Hollow when he was thirteen. Max is now twenty-five and zeroed in on expanding and going full speed ahead with the business. Then she rides into the prickly pears on her red motorcycle and turns his whole life into turmoil.

Lee Ann Brown's life has been bad, really bad, even her name isn't her own. It's given to her because she had no name, no family, just flung to the side like she was nothing. Now, after moving from family to family, she's in control and her and her motorcycle are free and on their own. She's learned to take up for herself, enjoy life as she wants to and no one's messing with her. Yep, she's seeing the USA and then the world one town at a time—until she has a flat in the middle of a prickly pear farm whose wild, beautiful colors drew her off-road.

And then, she sees him—the striking cowboy wrangling the prickly pears and his eyes turn to her, and things she's not expecting erupt inside and the fight is on.

Welcome back to Mule Hollow where love is still in the air—and the prickly pears. And the Matchmakin' Posse get that old song *Bad, Bad Leroy Brown* stuck in their head and see a gal whose determined to live life her way. But God's got a plan and the Matchmakers are in on it, full throttle. And sweet ole meddling Esther Mae wants a ride on the red motorcycle.

CHAPTER ONE

Satisfied at the sight surrounding him, Max Cantrell stood in the middle of his pasture full of his wonderful prickly pear cactus, its plum-toned fruit standing out like beacons. Life had taken him on a rugged road to bring him to this spot, but here he stood among his dream come true.

Who would have ever thought standing encircled by cactus topped off with ruby-toned tunas, the plump ball of fruit covered with clusters of tiny stickers that could dig deep no matter how tiny—just like things in life—he focused on his surroundings because here he stood among his prickly pear cactus. Stickers, yes but still they were the core of his dreams.

He was focusing on good things right now, not the

stickers of life that he could think of and get distracted by. Right now, he was standing among his beauties, knowing it was December, his favorite time of the year. Yes, Christmas was just a few weeks away and the most special time of the year, but harvesting his pears for jelly-making was next in line of the best of all times.

In a very roundabout way, when he was ten, he'd been given the gift of coming here to this small Texas town of Mule Hollow to live at the shelter called No Place Like Home. The shelter and the town were filled with blessings for those who needed them. And he and his mother had needed it all. Later, this cactus farm topped off everything when he was thirteen, giving him his destiny.

As odd as it sounded, life could be full of stickers, but his dreams came from burning the stickers off the cactus and setting free the beauty and taste of what was beneath those stickers. That too resembled the internal fight that simmered deep inside of him from his past, because of that, nothing was getting in the way of his vision for his future.

And that took patience because in the sizzling

summer heat, the cacti, with their bright yellow blossoms were amazing. Some had light pink blossoms that were outstanding—both marked the time from there to this moment in December. Those blooms lasted for a short time, then the blooms fell off and left the green ball covered in cactus needles, and the ripening began for the next few months until now. Early December, this deep ruby tone signaled it was time for fruit picking to begin.

Fruit picking then jelly production, and that was the time that produced his dreams for the future.

Thankfully, Texas weather still meant in December, it was often the high seventies temperature and perfect harvesting time. Next week was going to be great.

He smiled in satisfaction, everyone loved his jelly, and for that he was grateful.

This pasture of beautiful, bountiful cactus had given him a career he loved just as much as he loved the jelly. At twenty-five years old, he was a cowboy, something back in the day when he and his mom were homeless and he was sometimes sleeping in the car, it hadn't even crossed his mind that he'd become a cowboy or a prickly pear jelly maker. Especially who was to make his business, Mule Hollow Prickly Pear Jelly Company, a worldwide seller.

He'd been ten years old when he rode into Mule Hollow inside a van loaded with the ladies and their kids, all of them had taken the step to leave behind abusive husbands, boyfriends, and other things, and like his mom, had chosen a path of escape. And they'd ended up in a wonderful shelter, No Place Like Home, here in Mule Hollow, Texas.

The tiny town that had changed his life and others' lives too.

When he'd climbed out of that van, he hadn't been sure what in the world was going to happen. Then Cassie, a spunky young lady, had walked up and told him it was going to be okay, then a big-wheeled truck pulled up, driven by Jake, a young cowboy with eyes for Cassie. He'd looked out his open window and asked them if they wanted to go mudding. So, they climbed into the truck and had gone mudding, taking that big-wheeled truck of Jake's through some of the thickest, deepest mud Max had ever seen. And it had been addictive. Just like Mule Hollow.

And then later, after a lot of hard work and hanging in there, the mom he loved, the mom he would have and still would protect with his own life if needed, bought this small piece of property that was covered in the wild cactus, growing these amazing colored pears. She'd taught him how to make his grandmother's jelly, and now here he stood ready to hire and make a load of jelly. So much more had happened in his life since then, his father, who hadn't known he existed had shown up, won his mom's heart again, and they became a family. And now, here he stood ready to proceed.

With jelly making, nothing more despite living in a town that was known for matchmaking. No, he was happy the way he was and nothing more in his life was going to set him up for pain. He was in control now and ready to hire anyone who needed a job for a week picking the pears. Thankfully, he had a lineup ready to go.

His mom was worried about him and hoping he'd slack up and fall in love. No way. He had gals coming from all over thinking they'd dance with him at the town dances and he'd hand over his heart and forget his goals. Not happening, despite the fact that he'd been raised in the town that was famous because of the Matchmakin' Posse of Mule Hollow. *He* wasn't a catch despite living here.

But, those sweet, sneaky ladies matched cowboys and were good at it. Earlier in the year they helped match Luc and Izzy, the new hairstylist in town, and like all the other matches they'd made, Luc and Izzy were very happy.

The Matchmakers hadn't lost their touch, then again there was so much that went into making a match that he figured he was safe for a while. Sometimes young ladies came to town and put their radar on him so he took it with a smile and just had fun with it. But his own goals, his own agenda, was to be a cowboy business owner first and to take his prickly pear jelly company all over the country, then the world. So, the Mule Hollow matchmaking wasn't for him.

Freedom was what he liked.

His choices came first, and that was the way it

would remain. He got satisfaction when he worked this field, and there wasn't anything more beautiful than the plump rose cactus surrounding him right now. His future.

Not only that, but it gave him a way to give back by giving extra jobs to people before the Christmas shopping began. He knew from growing up that extra money during that time was a blessing. His pears did that for those who came to pick with him, and that gave him satisfaction like no other— Suddenly the roar of an engine signaled something was coming…what?

He cocked his head as he looked down the dirt road winding through the cactus that came from the country road to where he stood. And then he saw it, a motorcycle.

A motorcycle and a small rider—a woman.

She wore a deep red helmet and had a long, black braid swinging in the wind from one side to the other as she took in the colorful pears surrounding her. Who was this?

She came to a stop in front of a massive bunch of prickly pears and Max had instantly started moving her way as the red-topped gal swung her leg from one side and landed, standing beside the motorcycle. She was so focused, her hands on her hips, staring at the cactus surrounding her, that she hadn't yet seen him.

Max halted, stunned by her beauty as the tiny gal pulled the helmet from her head and like a lightning bolt striking a deep-rooted tree, the vision of her struck him and he slammed to a halt.

Then, the dark-haired beauty turned to face him, her dazzling blue eyes struck him like a slap to the face and he nearly fell on the prickly pears as she yelled, "Stop!"

He stopped, stunned, floored…

"Where did you come from?" she continued in a voice of warning, looking straight at him with an expression of the-fight-starts-here as her small fist came up, ready to battle.

Thundering heart and racing blood flowed through him. "I…was here when you came flying over that hill onto my property." At least his words were calm and on target—he wasn't sure about everything else inside him raging crazily. And it got worse as those eyes relaxed and an amazing smile spread across her beautiful face.

He wished his arm was still on the fence post because he almost fell in among the prickly cactus the moment those eyes of hers sparkled—the woman had eyes to die for *or worse, to send him falling straight in a herd of cactus stickers.*

* * *

Fist up, Lee Ann Brown dared the cowboy to even think he was coming closer. He wasn't wearing a hat, but he looked like a cowboy, black wavy hair, light green toned long-sleeved shirt that wasn't tucked into faded jeans, that were tucked into a pair of weathered brown leather boots.

This was a long, tall Texan and a handsome one at that—*and why had that thought popped into her defensive thoughts?*

Yes, the cowboy was stunning, amazingly handsome, and her noticing that was astonishing because *she* was never drawn to a man. And never, ever planned to be.

She was a single gal who had a past that ensured that she always would be single, alone, and on her own.

So, why, as the handsome cowboy came her way, were these odd thoughts, for the first time ever, crossing her mind like an approaching threat?

Hands up, he hitched his brow. "I'm Max Cantrell, and this is *my* property. Are you looking for help?"

He owned the land she was trespassing on so she lowered her fist. "Sorry, I'm Lee Ann Brown. I was driving by and the prickly pears distracted me, I reacted by coming up this road without thinking." He grinned and her stomach rolled so she pushed her words out, "My brain was locked on these *beautiful* plum-toned fruits on the cactus that are surrounding us right now."

"My cactus will do that to people. Plus, they make great jelly.

Shock rushed through her. "You mean like the Mule Hollow Prickly Pear Jelly Company?" Surely she hadn't stumbled on the place she wanted to see?

"This is it. You've heard of it?"

"Yes, and it is an amazing-tasting jelly."

"For smiles like yours after eating our jelly, that's why I work really hard to make it special. The recipe came from my grandmother. It's a long story, but I'm glad I'm able to make it and let it represent her."

His words dug deep. He represented his grandmother with love. She'd never known her grandmother. Or her mother. Or her dad—*move on.* "Well, she'd be proud is all I can say, because I was heading to Mule Hollow, and I was also going to see if I could find the cactus farm where that amazing jelly was produced from. But I didn't realize I was driving down the road straight to it. I didn't even realize it when I drove down this dirt road, there was no gate up there to stop me. All I saw was the beauty of the fruit and here I came. Did I miss the sign?"

"Nah. I haven't put one up. Not many people come looking at cacti or cactus as most Texans call it. But they love the jelly and for that I'm grateful. Also, if they came, they might reach out and touch it and get the dreaded sting of the stickers. The stickers are almost invisible and it's the dickens to get them out of your fingers. Texans know that, most of them, so I don't worry about a gate. I come and go and I have a lot of people who are fixin' to come help me pick the fruit next week."

Excitement shot through her. "It's *that* time?"

"Yes, it is. It's that time." His eyes lit up.

She wanted to pick them but didn't know how long she was going to be here. But she worked jobs, *all* kinds of jobs in every different place she stayed at. She waitressed a lot, but did other things too, helped remodel a house, carried food to people in need through a group she learned about. She'd worked in stores, and she'd worked whatever it took to keep her mind creative and keep her money up, making travel possible. Getting on the road again was always her target. But picking prickly pear pulled hard at making her stay here in Mule Hollow for more than a day—which she needed to head to town.

"I better head out. I'm stopping in Mule Hollow to look around. I want to see the pink hair salon and eat at Sam's Diner—maybe hear *Great Balls Of Fire* or *Blue Suede Shoes* playing. That juke box is world-renowned. Maybe I'll spot those Matchmakers—not that I'm looking for a match, but they're historic and it would be fun to see if they look like Molly Popp's descriptions. But I'm not look'n for a match."

"If you're not looking, you can get the message across with your attitude. I'm not looking either and they get the message, since they've sent gals my way but I just have fun with it and don't take the bait."

"Great to know. See you later—"

"But—wait, you have a flat."

"A flat." She spun around and stared in disbelief at her flat tire. It was flat as a fritter—she didn't even know where she'd heard that description but it fit perfectly. "How did this happen?"

He moved to stand beside her, at his close presence she shot him a glance then looked back at the bike like he was doing. "Sometimes you can get something in your tire and it takes its time deflating. But I can guarantee you my prickly pears didn't cause that. They're prickly but they won't deflate a tire."

"That's good to know. Now to figure out where to get it fixed."

"Come on, I'll drive you to town. We've got a great wrecker service in town owned by Prudy. He's been around for many years, him and his ancient wrecker. He'll come pick it up and then fix the tire and get you back on the road."

She just stared at him. He was a great cowboy, a hero—she was not looking for a hero—despite *how* great he was.

Nope, she was looking to keep her life to herself, enjoy what she wanted to enjoy and not get sidetracked or attached to anyone. Definitely not get sidetracked by finding this cowboy handsome or appealing. Just helpful and that was as far as she would let her thoughts go—then she realized they were standing close, staring at each other.

Just staring. Not moving but her heart shot to pounding as his gaze dropped to her lips and then back to her eyes. Hers did the same before returning to his face.

His hand went to his jaw. "Is there something on my face?"

His face—"No, I'm just getting my mind on what I'll do next. And that's riding into town with you and getting Prudy to rescue me. I mean rescue my motorcycle."

And that was the truth.

CHAPTER TWO

Max couldn't help glancing over in the passenger seat at the motorcycle rider—*beautiful* motorcycle rider. She'd placed her leather saddle bags and her helmet in between them like a line drawn in the seat.

Around Mule Hollow they had more women than there used to be but still the town was low on single women. A new woman in town was going to grab attention. There were cowgirls, business women— regular ladies, but no motorcycle riders. Sure, there were gals who came to the town events but he didn't know what they did since he tried not to interact with them all that much.

Now when they did things to draw his attention,

like wrestling a greased-up pig, he couldn't help but get a laugh or two with them. Actually, a lot of good had come from the pig wresting events, and as out of the normal as pig wrestling was he found a woman riding into town on a motorcycle more attention-drawing.

There was a true tale about the gal who rode into town after Molly Popp wrote an article featuring single cowboy Bob Jacobs in her famous newspaper column. That was before Molly and Bob knew they were destined for each other and she brought a herd of women to town intent on marrying him. One of them was the motorcycle lady, and the laughable stories about what had happened on that motorcycle visit had Max labeling all motorcycle-riding ladies way off limit. Not that he'd been looking, but right now, he was looking at Lee Ann Brown and his head was spinning in a whole different way.

Max's gaze was drawn to Lee Ann Brown—a motorcycle-riding lady. He knew there were ladies who enjoyed riding motorcycles, he'd just never been attracted to— He shut that kick-in-the-gut thought down. He wasn't looking for attraction in his life right now. Mule Hollow held events that brought ladies to town looking for a cowboy to fall in love with, and he kept himself away from connection. Despite that, there were some who had him on their target list. Some had participated in the last pig wrestling event and the Posse—the Matchmakin' Posse—had him on a horse in the arena to help rescue those who got in trouble. They'd had hopes he'd rescue one of the gals and fall in love. Not happening, he put his smiles on for them but his walls were up. It did happen for Luc Asher that night when he'd rode in and rescued Izzy. Thankfully their romance took the focus off of him for a while.

Sure, temptations were everywhere, but he worked hard to ignore simple attractions that could mess up his focus on his future. He was the kid who had grown up not knowing he even had a dad, wondering what happened to his dad and wondering if his mom had had a wild streak there before he was born. Nothing crazy like that was going to come out to change his focus because of a one-night mistake that he could make. His mom and dad's moment had come out good in the end, but for him there had been hard-learned lessons from it.

Lessons he would never let occur in his life simply for a moment of fun.

He didn't think about it often, but something about this motorcyclist had his attention and her name, Lee Ann Brown.

Trouble… The jukebox at Sam's Diner played old songs and one of them was *Bad, Bad Leroy Brown,* so Max heard that song often. It didn't always pop up but it was there. Now, he had Lee Ann Brown in the truck and as much as he didn't want it to, that song kept playing in his head. Except it was Bad, Bad *Lee Ann* Brown playing and he couldn't get it out of his mind.

He focused on the road, his hands gripped the steering wheel as he fought to get his brain straight. Lee Ann Brown was bad for him, but not the way the song insinuated. But, now that he thought about it, she did look spunky, and she'd said she could take care of herself, so she might just be bad, bad, Lee Ann Brown— and as much as he didn't want it to, that drew him even more.

She'd said she could take up for herself, said she didn't have anything to be afraid—so she was confident she could take care of herself. Maybe she'd been through some stuff, like he had or maybe worse.

"I usually carry some flat fixing supplies, but they're not in my bag. And to be honest, I've been riding this motorcycle for the last several years and I've never had a flat before. I've never driven among prickly pears either. But I just don't think those tiny stickers would flatten my tire."

He grinned, he couldn't help it. "You're right about that. Tires are thicker than our skin, so you picked up whatever poked that hole in your tire somewhere along the way, not from my prickly pear cactus. Probably a nail or a screw along the way, that's what it looks like to me. So, somewhere along the road you ran over it and the air probably slowly eased out until it leaked out and it went flat. Riding through the uneven dirt road could have worked it out after being on pavement."

He glanced at her and found her looking at him with a serious look on her face—he wondered if she ever laughed very much.

"You're probably right, I picked it up somewhere along the way."

"Prudy, our wrecker driver, will be happy to pick it up for you. If anybody can get you a tire, Prudy can. May not be today though. You might be stranded for a few days."

She looked away, tapped her short nails on the door panel as if that brain of hers was thinking. Automatically his brain wondered what the bad, bad Lee Ann Brown was thinking. It hit him then that she might have been picked on about that growing up. Why would her parents have given her a name so close to that song?

"There are places you can stay," he said, needing to assure her and get his brain off of where it was at the moment. "We've got some bed and breakfasts around. I'm sure you can find a place to stay. Also, there's a lot of great ladies in town who are plenty happy to lend a room if needed."

Instantly, the Posse popped into his brain, if they saw him with Lee Ann, he had a feeling they were going to zero in on him since he was the one who found her. They had a thing about first meetings. Those minds of theirs would target him like never before. This was a bad, *bad* time for him, that's all he had to say about it as the tune played through his brain.

Gracious, he couldn't get it out of his head—he needed to talk. "Okay, so while we make this long drive toward town, you see the pink dot there at the end of nine miles. That's Lacy's place, Heavenly Inspirations, and all the other colored buildings surrounding it will slowly come into view the closer we get. It's nine miles from here to there. People always talk about it and well, I can't help but wonder if you get asked—" Not where he'd planned to go. "I mean, you know." He couldn't finish as her head tilted toward him and her eyes had a definite don't-go-there look. She knew exactly what he was attempting to say.

He held a hand up from the steering wheel. "I didn't mean to irritate you. It's just, well, you drive a motorcycle, you wear a leather jacket and a helmet, and something tells me you're tough." He laughed, just a huff of a laugh before he shut it down. Her eyes widened even more as her glare intensified. "You obviously get that song sang to you a lot."

Her fingers that had been tapping on the door panel now hammered before she yanked her hand away and slapped it onto her thigh. He yanked his gaze away and focused on the road but then his eyes were locked on those amazing blue eyes that were still glaring at him.

Then she sighed, letting it out slowly, he tore his gaze off of her and back to the road.

"Yes," she gritted out. "I'm bad, bad *Lee Ann* Brown. I've lived with that name ever since they picked me up from the side of the road as an infant. Some crazy person in the program who gives out names was probably having fun that day. Probably listening to that song on the radio when they walked in carrying me, a tiny baby covered up in a borrowed blanket. And like now, I probably had an angry look on my face. I can only imagine, even though I don't remember it, I have a feeling whoever that person was took one look at me, and despite me being a girl, she named me Lee Ann Brown. And I do, just so you know, live up to the name if needed."

Floored by her words he slowed the truck. "I'm so sorry, Lee Ann."

"Don't be. I am who I am,"

Yes, she was. "I believe you. I bet nobody messes

with you."

"Not for *long*. They may decide to try it, and *plenty* have, but they quit pretty quick. Even as a kid the jokes stopped and now it gets ended almost as soon as a serious jerk starts the picking."

She was one tough cookie, but he wondered if it was as easy as she portrayed it to be.

Change of subject… "Mule Hollow is known for its wonderful people, and they're going to enjoy you. And yeah, they might ask you about your name like I did. They probably can't help it, and that's probably what happens. But I can guarantee you, they won't pick on you about it. As a matter of fact, I have a feeling, I got one woman in my mind almost instantly, Esther Mae Wilcox is going to love it. She's a huge fan of that song."

"How do you know that?"

He grinned, glad she sounded a little less tense. "Sam's Diner has an ancient jukebox. It's got old songs on it that come from that era or thereabouts. And it's odd, real odd, because half the time it plays what it wants to. Not what buttons someone poked into it."

"I'd heard that from people talking about the town."

"Yep, you've heard of Lacy Brown, she's the one who put that pink salon in and got everyone involved in painting the town the bright colors. It looks like a happy rainbow, saying, 'Welcome. Come on in and have fun.' She drove into town in her pink Caddy and went to Sam's, put her money in the jukebox and pushed the button to Elvis's *Blue Suede Shoes* but it chose to play *Great Balls of Fire* instead. And she is like a great ball of fire in spirit, joined up with the Posse, turned up the heat, and saved this dying town."

He chuckled as her face lit up. "I like that song. And even though I'm only twenty-four, I like the fire of that song."

"It's played other songs and yours is one of them— you know what I mean. Izzy Cranberry *Asher*, now, had a song from her grannies playing in her head when she came to town. The tune of the *Green Acres* television show was playing in her head, but instead of the words green acres, Mule Hollow took their place along with adapted lyrics that her grandmothers sang."

"Really?"

He couldn't help hitching his brows. "They sang it in her head and got her here to Mule Hollow. So, I have a feeling, *Bad, Bad Leroy Brown* is about to ring in everybody's head now that you're in town."

She studied the town on the horizon that was arriving quickly, thank goodness. His heart was doing odd things like slamming against his ribs as those eyes had a look that said she wished she could just be simple Lee Ann Thompson. Or Lee Ann Mulberry, Le*Ann* Rimes—that woman could sing but this was Lee Ann Brown.

He smiled as her name played to the tune in his head. "I like your name and I've got a feeling it comes in handy for you in certain situations. You look tough, Lee Ann. And I think that's a good thing if you're riding across country on that motorcycle of yours all by your lonesome."

Her fingers went back to tapping on the door panel but her expression softened instead of hardened, and— *gracious*—his heart slammed against his chest at the softness he saw spread over her face.

It was a softness *far more dangerous* than the bad, bad Lee Ann Brown look.

CHAPTER THREE

Lee Ann stared at the town coming into view, relief and excitement mixed inside her chest. She needed something to focus on other than Max.

That was like a kick in the knee—she was actually more excited than she had thought she'd be. She wasn't even on her motorcycle and she was happy. She was riding in the truck with this handsome cowboy. And she liked it—*no*, she liked this beautiful *town* on the horizon.

That's what she liked.

All the different colors splashed across the skyline, the hot pink hair salon was the obvious focus point since it stood out like a pink lightning bolt—a *lightning bolt*—of all things to think about. She looked back at him as the bolt shot through her—"It *is* amazing," she gushed, louder than needed, then rattled on, "It's just as cool as I've heard. I don't know why in all the years I've been traveling on my motorcycle that I never came here before. I mean, I've traveled to several states and loved every moment, but this time I came back to Texas to check out Mule Hollow after so many people asked me about it. I'd never been here so here I am riding in this truck into the tiny town everyone loves that's in my *home* state."

"Welcome."

The laughter in his voice drew her and she shot him a don't-get-too-cocky look. "Thanks, but I'm *not* looking for a relationship."

His dark brows dipped together. "*Me* either." They stared at each other then, thankfully, he had to look back at the road as he continued, "There's Prudy's gas station at the end of the road. He'll go get your motorcycle with his wrecker, and I can take you to Lacy's or Sam's and they can help find you a place to stay."

"Thanks."

They drove past the first building. Her heart was

raging. *Raging.* The town was beautiful with every store painted a different color. Bright yellow at the end, she could see it, she knew that was the famous Pete's Feed and Seed, and then there was just store after store.

"This is going to be fun. I'm glad I came. So, yes, I'll find a place to stay, get a job for a few days, if there are any. That's what I do, travel around and take jobs that support me while I'm roaming. It gives me money to travel to the next place."

"You just move from place to place?"

"Yes. I have no ties, nothing to hold me down. It's the way I like it." She looked at him as it struck her. "I'm always looking for something different to do, so if you've got a job opening for picking prickly pears, I'd love to hire on."

* * *

She wanted him to hire her! "Sure thing," he said, his brain ticking wildly. "You'll enjoy it, if you like adventure like you say you do. I have to warn you that you could get stuck with the prickly stickers."

"Stickers don't stop me. I can promise you that."

He had a feeling nothing stopped her. "Then you're hired." He pulled to a stop at the ancient garage and gas station that hadn't changed in all these years. He didn't even know how old Prudy was, but the old guy loved what he did. He was sitting in a chair in front of the glass window, and his ancient wrecker, which he'd picked many a car and truck up with over the years, sat off to the side.

"Howdy," Prudy said, grinning as he ambled over to Lee Ann's open window. "Pretty lady, I've never seen you in town before. Welcome."

"Hi. I'm Lee Ann and I'm glad to be here. I rode my motorcycle into town. Well, before I got to town, I got to this cowboy's place and had a flat among the cactus. Can you go pick up my motorcycle out of his prickly pear patch and fix it for me?"

Prudy's smile stretched big across his wrinkled face. "Well, *sure* I can. That's what I do. That old wrecker is always tweaked and ready to go. It can roll with the best of them. You just tell me which prickly pear patch and I'll go get it, then fix that tire for you.

You and this cowboy need to go for breakfast at Sam's. I hear all the ladies are over there, you know, having their mid-morning coffee."

"That's where we're heading," he assured Prudy. He told the older man where to find her motorcycle, and then he drove them to the first vacant parking space and pulled in. She was out of the truck the moment it was in park. He hopped out and met her on the wooden sidewalk, and beat her to the door. His mom would have his hide if he didn't open the door for a lady. He pulled it open and smiled. "After you, and get ready for whatever they toss your way." He hitched a half grin and prepared himself for the same thing because they were entering Sam's Diner together and that was going to cause a ruckus.

* * *

Seeing the odd look in Max's eyes as he held the door open for her, Lee Ann wasn't sure what was up as she passed him and entered the diner. And then she was instantly overwhelmed by the old, historic-looking place, but it was the people inside that got her. They were talking, smiling, and enjoying each other, and it slammed into her. Max obviously was worried about something she wasn't aware of, but she loved the scene.

Loved seeing people happy being friends. She didn't let *herself* live it but she enjoyed seeing it in other people. They were all looking happy as they all ate and talked. He was probably worried about rumors they might create walking in together.

The instant she looked around her attention went to the two old men sitting at the table by the window. Applegate Thornton and Stanley Orr. The checker players everyone talked about.

She walked straight their way, Max trailing behind her. She couldn't help grinning. "Hi, I'm Lee Ann, and I just got to Mule Hollow, but I've heard a lot about y'all from all the people all over the country who read Molly Popp's articles. You're definitely recognizable from her descriptions." She reached out her hand to the lean, tall, grouchy-looking old guy with a face that was as skinny as a pine pole and bushy eyebrows underneath his crooked Stetson. "It's nice to meet you, App." He shook her hand and studied her.

"Same. You're spunky."

She laughed. "Sometimes." Then she held her now free hand out to the cute, chubby fella. "Nice to meet you too, Stanley Orr, both of you guys."

"Glad to meet you," Stanley said, hitching his full lips up, his eyes twinkling. "Now, if you read about us in Molly Popp's articles, then you know my partner here, he's a grumpy old dude, but not as grumpy as he used to be. But we are a little older than when Molly started her articles. I'm still beating him in checkers if you want to know the truth. But we're glad you're here."

She grinned and asked, "Who's winning?"

"Me," Applegate grunted.

Stanley rolled his eyes. "I'm winning this game, App just ain't acceptin' it."

They were as grumpy old fellas as Molly's articles made them out to be—it was awesome. She grinned. "Y'all are as grumpy as Molly said y'all are."

"Yes, they are," a plump lady with bright red hair, sparkling eyes, and a wide grin called from the booth across the room.

"You're Esther Mae Wilcox."

"Bingo, you're right," the overall-wearing lady with the gray, frizzy hair said with a wide-faced grin. Her smile was almost as big as, well, a basketball.

"It's nice to meet you too, Norma Sue Jenkins," she said striding over to the booth where the ladies sat. Her gaze landed on the pretty lady sitting in the booth beside Norma Sue. She was just as dainty as Molly had described her. The whitest hair, the most beautiful sapphire eyes that twinkled with kindness. "You're Adela Ledbetter and as pretty and kind as Molly said you were."

"Well, thank you. We're excited you're in town, and you rode in with Max?"

"Well, I was coming to Mule Hollow because I travel. I travel everywhere. I ride a motorcycle and that's all I do. I work while I'm in a town and then I travel to the next town or state."

"You don't live *anywhere*?" Norma Sue asked, strong emphasis on anywhere.

"No, I sure don't." She got that question a lot. "I'm from Texas but I just love seeing the world and I'm working my way around it. *But* everywhere I go when someone learns I'm from Texas, they ask me if I've been to Mule Hollow. Why?" She grinned. "Because they read Molly Popp's articles."

Esther Mae chuckled. "That gal can write."

"Yes, she can. I've been traveling for almost five years now, and I decided it was time to come check this place out. Especially since I love prickly pear jelly and Mule Hollow is getting known for that on *top* of marrying cowboys off—which I'm *not* here to do."

Adela looked at Lee Ann, and then her bright blue gaze shifted past Lee Ann. "So, that's how you and Max ended up coming to town together. You came to see his farm."

Max—she glanced over her shoulder and saw Max talking to the checker players, giving her space. She looked back at the curious ladies. "I got detoured. I was on my way to town and I got sidetracked. I love back roads and took one and ended up seeing the cactus, and I turned down the bumpy dirt road that weaved through them and was just enchanted. They are beautiful. I couldn't help it, I got off my bike, trespassing to check them out, and then I saw Max walking toward me through the cactus. We started talking and I found out who he was, and found out I had a flat on the property of the Mule Hollow Prickly Pear Jelly Company. I was amazed. By the flat and where I was at the place with the most *amazing* jelly ever.”

“Sorry about your flat,” Norma Sue said as they were all watching her and she saw others sitting around them were watching too.

“It’s fine. Prudy’s fixing it,” she said and kept going. “And now I’m here at Sam’s Diner, where I can’t wait to plug in a quarter in the jukebox and play Norma Sue’s favorite song, *Great Balls of Fire*—”

“*No way*,” Norma Sue growled. “Please, don’t play that song. I’ve worked on that jukebox so many times and it still likes that song best of all. Everybody knows it gets stuck. And like you, *every* new person pushes that button just to cause me trouble.”

She laughed. She loved this and was so glad she’d come. “I hate to tell you, but I’m going to have to play it. A person can’t come to Sam’s Diner without hearing that song and wanting to get up and dance to it.”

"I don't," Norma Sue huffed.

"Oh hush, Norma. I *like* what Lee Ann's saying," Esther Mae said, grinning big. "I especially like the part you said about that you ride a motorcycle. I've always dreamed of riding on a motorcycle. And you know, we've only ever had that one motorcycle rider that came to town, and well, I wasn't going to ask that one woman for a ride on her motorcycle. I just couldn't wait for her to get out of town, but I'm going to ask you. You look like you know how to ride that thing. You've got room on the back?"

Stunned, Lee Ann had no words for the moment. The entire diner went silent. Not a conversation was happening anywhere. Not a sound and one scan about the room and she saw everyone had their eyes on her. Needing a way out she sought out Max but he hitched a brow and the dude's eyes were twinkling with humor.

Yep, she'd walked herself into an Esther Mae Wilcox problem.

"Well…I do have a second seat on my bike. I don't have an extra helmet though, and you *have* to wear a helmet." There was her way out.

The redhead squealed. "I'll *get me a helmet*. Heck, I can drive all the way to Ranger and get me a helmet. If I do that, we're on." She gave Lee Ann a thumbs up as the entire diner exploded in laughter.

And Lee Ann knew she was trapped. She was going to *have* to take Esther Mae Wilcox on a motorcycle ride.

She just had to hope Esther Mae wouldn't squeeze her so hard she exploded while driving. Or she wouldn't say something so funny it threw her off balance as she laughed.

Seriously, her thoughts rolled—they could do more than have a flat like she'd had coming into town. They could *crash* into a cactus or a huge tree—

"*Wellll*," a little short man drawled, as he came striding up, his bowed legs giving him a swagger. This was Sam, short, wrinkled, bowlegged, and—breaking into her troubled thoughts. "Is it on?"

Glad for the distraction and knowing who he was, his grin and the look in his eyes said he knew exactly the position she had just crammed herself into.

"It looks like we've got something to look forward to. Watching Esther Mae ride on the back of your motorcycle is gonna be fun to watch. Are you excited about it?" He hitched a bushy brow.

Excited—"Um, sure. I've never taken a challenge before and this isn't really a challenge, this is a—"

"A fun event," Max said from beside her.

She slung her head to the side and caught him grinning.

He continued, "All the folks in Mule Hollow enjoy seeing unusual things happen. Watching *you* carry sweet Esther Mae for a ride on the back of your red motorcycle is going to be *real* fun to watch." His eyes twinkled with teasing.

Teasing that zipped through her like the surprise it was. The cowboy was teasing her.

"*Red*," Esther Mae squealed. "*I* get to ride on a *red* motorcycle? I can't wait. This is going to be so exciting. Oh *so, so, sooo* exciting."

Norma Sue slapped the table with her hand. "Yep, this is gonna be a show. I'll tell you what, we'll go get that helmet today. Then we can set this up for everybody to watch. Either tomorrow after church or later. How's that sound?" The kinky-headed woman gave her a direct look that said there's-no way-of-getting-out-of-this-now.

Lee Ann sighed inside, but first things first. "Okay, but I just got to town and I don't even have a place to stay tonight."

"I've got you," a small, spunky-looking woman called as she leaned out of her booth. "I have an open room at my bed and breakfast."

"You'll love it," Esther Mae gushed. "Polly's place is wonderful."

Lee Ann's brain clicked. "You're Pollyanna, and you opened a B&B—and fell in love with your neighbor." She grinned, remembering people talking about the fun story. "This is wild that I'm standing here after hearing all the stories Molly wrote in her articles, and I'm recognizing you. It's fun realizing who you each are. And yes, I would *love* to rent a room from you. I'd want to meet that wrinkled dog, Bogie, too. And do you still have your parrot? Everyone talks about the singing bird almost as much as they talk about Samantha the donkey." She laughed, realizing how much she actually knew about this town.

Pollyanna smiled. "They're all there. But Pepper is a cockatiel not a parrot. He's a very mischievous, singing bird that loves visitors. So, believe me, he'll sing to you until you leave. And our sweet Bogie is still with us too. I'm about to leave and you can get this handsome cowboy standing beside you to bring you out when you're ready."

"Great," Norma Sue said as she patted the table. "Now, everybody, get back to eating and let's let Max and Lee Ann find a table and order something to eat. *Sam*, have at it, dude. Give this lady something to eat because I'm sure after reading all those articles about you and about us, that she's got something on her mind."

Lee Ann grinned. "Actually, I do. I want something specific."

"And what will that be?" Sam grinned.

"I love prickly pear jelly, and by coincidence ended up running into the prickly pear jelly cowboy and his pears." She grinned at Max. "He brought me to the diner and got Prudy to go pick up my bike so I think this calls for some wonderful toast with some of Max's prickly pear jelly, please."

Sam's grin grew big. "You got it. Sausage and eggs too?"

"Yes, sounds wonderful."

"You two take that table right there." He pointed to the one on the other side of the café across the aisle from Applegate and Stanley. "Coffee? Tea?"

"Coffee and water, please." She strode to where Sam had pointed and slid into the booth.

"I'll have the same, Sam." Max slid in across from her, grinning.

What a grin he had. She'd somehow ridden her motorcycle into a whole new world, and she was going to have to adjust—especially to this cowboy and his amazing grin.

She liked that grin, those eyes—*halt!*

Lee Ann took a breath—attempting to adjust her brain and get it back in line.

CHAPTER FOUR

Max wasn't sure what to do after they sat down at the table. Everyone was watching them, some bluntly, like App and Stanley from four feet away. The Posse was watching intently from across the diner, and many other eyes he could feel from cowboys he knew were at various tables.

Some were pretending they weren't watching but were.

Sam at least had given them a bit of space from the ladies when he'd placed them across the diner at this table.

Heart thrashing erratically like a bucking bull as he looked at the beauty sitting across from him. This outrageous attraction he felt was an unusual feeling for him. Feeling the eyes of the Posse and everyone else on him was rough too, but he didn't know how to get rid of any of it at the moment.

Suddenly, as if his thinking about the Posse brought them to life, Esther Mae sprang from her booth and headed their way at a rapid pace.

And an odd look on her face. "I just realized you never told us your last name. I don't know why, but in my head, I'm suddenly hearing that song, Leroy Brown. You know, *Bad, Bad, Leroy Brown*. You're so cute in your motorcycle outfit and your black hair, it just suddenly has me wanting to turn on the jukebox."

The stunned look on Lee Ann's face slammed into Max. It also hit him that she hadn't told them her last name and he realized it was on purpose. He'd missed that until now. She however was used to the reaction her name got. He felt, as he looked at her, that she didn't care for it.

"Actually, that is my name. I'm Lee Ann Brown," she said, the words stiff then determined and the entire diner went quiet as she looked around defiantly. "I ride a motorcycle and I'm one tough cookie. I try as *hard* as possible to live up to the song that has followed me around ever since I was a kid."

There was no fun in her voice as the words rolled out. They were words she obviously had grown used to saying.

"Oh, honey bunny," Esther Mae gushed, not looking at all turned off from that look of defense on Lee Ann's face. "Don't be all upset. I tell you, if I was going to get named, *especially* if I was riding a motorcycle around the country like you have been, it's a great name. It's kind of a standoffish name, you know what I mean? And, you're small, but you look tough."

"I am."

Esther Mae grinned. "Well, if I lifted weights, I would probably be a heavy weightlifter. You know what I mean? I could probably look really tough with this red hair of mine, but that's not me. I try to be a sweet lady. I like bright clothes and I like to make people laugh. But, I see right now, I'm not making you laugh, if I offended you, I am so sorry. *Still,* I love that song and if you ride all over the country you need to be tough, honey. You, that motorcycle, and that song just goes together in a good way."

He saw the intake of the "good way" as Lee Ann took the words in.

Esther Mae grinned and continued, "I'm going to go play it… If the jukebox obeys me. Sometimes it won't. It likes a few other songs, so I'm not guaranteeing that it's going to play. I had a feeling you're probably hoping I don't get it to play. But I can't help it. Lee Ann Brown, *I'm* going to ride a motorcycle tomorrow, so to celebrate, I'm going to put this quarter in the jukebox." She held a quarter up, then grinning broadly she hurried over and plopped it in the slot. Then she poked a number with her pointer finger, spun around grinning as *Bad, Bad, Leroy Brown* roared to life on the ancient jukebox.

And everybody started clapping.

Esther Mae gave a thumbs up then hurried back to her table—thank goodness. The room quietened as Max looked at the beauty sitting across from him, needing to clarify Esther Mae's actions. "That sweet woman loves adventure, she loves helping people and she's good at figuring people out. For some reason, I have a feeling she's doing that right now. Figuring you out. Hope you don't get mad at her. Even though the song bugs you, it goes with you, at least what I've seen of you. Is there somebody else hiding underneath that vibrant I'm-a-strong-gal camouflage you've got on?"

Her gaze flickered as she took a short breath, glanced from him to the side, and he knew she was probably looking at Applegate and Stanley, who had gone back to playing checkers, but he knew their ears were on alert. Those two were supposedly near deaf but miraculously they had always been able to hear what they wanted to hear. Could be powerful hearing aids that had advanced over the last few years. Or they weren't as hard of hearing as they said they were.

However, he and obviously Lee Ann knew too that there was a chance if spoken too loud her words would be heard. Then, her gaze came back to him, softer, and his heart fluttered for that look this time. She had strength and vulnerability and he saw it.

Sam brought their breakfast, giving her a moment as Sam grinned then got out of the way.

She leaned forward and in a low, raspy voice, said,

"Look, I'm bad, like I told you. Yeah, I got things in my past that I don't like to talk about and I'm not planning on talking about them. None of it matters anyway. Me, I live my life for me, day for day, mile for mile. Yeah, I love the Lord. I *am* a Christian. *He's* gotten me as far as I am, but *He* also gave me permission to be me. And that's who I am, me. Tough, blunt, determined to make it on my own, with God's help."

She lifted her finger when he started to talk and he shut up. "No, I don't always do what I should do, but *He* made me. He gave me this unruly life so I'm not apologizing about anything."

Whoa, Max liked this gal and there was no denying it.

He leaned forward, looking deep into those no-backing-down eyes of hers. "I'm that way too. I've had a lot of things in my life that could help determine how I live and who I am. From when I was a kid to where and *who* I am now and where I'm heading. Yeah, I'm a Christian too, but I can tell you just because we're Christians doesn't mean we don't have lumps and huge caved-in spots in the roads of our life."

His heart thundered, they were both leaning toward each other and they stared eye to eye. Then, still leaning toward him, she picked up her fork and stabbed it into her eggs.

He kept going in a heavy low-toned voice for only her. "My mother had a rough life, but dug out of major issues and I watched her. I watched blessings come from them too. Just getting my dad back, the dad I never even knew I had, was the biggest blessing for me and Mom—and then finding Mule Hollow has been a life changer. Just so you know, you're in a great place right now, relax. Let some of the tension I see loose and have a good time. Because I have a feeling you do like me, live one day at a time focused on where you want to go, me too."

They stared at each other, she let go of her fork as something between them tightened like a rubber band. She leaned back and he leaned back in his chair and that rubber band stretched, it's like they were both fighting the tension of it.

He held strong because he suddenly knew if that rubber band broke, wow, she would be in his arms, the table would fly, and he would be trying to see if those firm, determined lips of hers would soften up between his.

What, he didn't want that. Even if he did want that, it wasn't happening unless she wanted it. He'd *never* stepped across those bounds.

She slapped her fingers on the table and drummed a beat or two. Then, thank goodness, Sam walked up with their drinks that he hadn't brought earlier. He set them on the table between them, put his hands on his hips and grinned at them. "Now you two need to relax just a little bit. You know and I know that y'all are being watched, and I can tell you the heat from the lightning of this raging storm between the two of you is hot and noticeable. If I can see it, they can see it." He rolled his eyes in the direction of the Matchmakin' Posse. "Now, don't let the food get cold." Then he was gone.

Max saw Lee Ann's gaze go across the room and then back to him. He wondered if she was telling her heartbeat to slow down like he was demanding his do. No matter what, they needed to eat and get out of the diner.

He needed to drop her off at the bed and breakfast and drive away fast.

And he needed to do it soon.

* * *

Lee Ann and Max had barely spoken after leaving the diner, and she could tell he was just as eager to get away from her as she was to get away from him.

She needed to get checked into her room, then figure out how in the world to take Esther Mae on a motorcycle ride safely. She had a feeling that the woman was going to hop on the back end of her motorcycle and tell her to put the pedal to the metal. Truth was, Lee Ann loved doing that, but she wasn't doing it with Esther Mae Wilcox riding on the back end and everybody in town watching. Nope, nada, *no* way.

They arrived at the beautiful house, a three-story ancient home from she wasn't sure when, but it was amazing. She stepped out of that truck taking her bags and helmet with her, totally infatuated, when suddenly a short-haired, wrinkled, reddish-brown dog raced around the corner of the house charging her way. He had a big mouth spread wide, exposing a mass of teeth, wrinkles around his neck that shook with each pounding of his paws on the ground while every other part of the two-foot tall body was pure muscle.

As if to prove he was an awesome dog five feet from her, he sprang into the air. Nearly *five* feet into the air he sailed, then tossing his rump to the side as if to get her to try and tap him before he landed back on the ground. She should have been terrified but instead she laughed—he was great.

Behind him a grinning young man, maybe a little younger than Max, barreled around the house chasing the dog. "*Bogie,* slow down, old man." He waved his arms at her. "It's okay, he won't hurt you. *Protect* you, but not hurt you. He was just excited when he heard y'all drive up. And he's testing you to see if you can give him a tap on the rump before he landed and raced into another wide circle around you."

Exactly what she'd thought.

"Hey, Gil. Your dog loves to fly," Max said, reaching out a hand and shaking the dog owner's. "Glad you're home from college for the weekend."

"Me too. I head back tomorrow but you know me, I try to come home as often as I can to check on Bogie. He's lived a long life for a Shar Pei, and I want to see him as often as possible before I lose him."

"I get it," Max said. "He's a great dog. I wish they had longer lives."

"He's actually done better than most. He's almost eleven years old and eight years is stretching their lifespan. But here he goes flying through the air. This keeps him in shape and he's fighting old age all the way."

As he said those words the beautiful muscled dog leaped into the air again and sailed straight toward Lee Ann. She watched, amazed, then the dog swung his hips so they sailed past his head toward her then he landed on the ground just a foot away from her and charged away. He was on the run in a wide circle of the huge yard. Amazing.

"He's coming again," Gil said. "Try and tap his hips, it's his challenge to you and those he's making friends with.

She grinned. "I'll give it a go."

Then Bogie flew into the air once more, tossed his rump her way and now knowing what he was doing, Lee Ann quickly reached out and tapped him on the rump. She laughed as the dog landed, spun, and came to sit at her feet, looking up at her with his amazing dark eyes. Eyes that called to her.

She dropped to her knees and set her bags and helmet down, Bogie cocked his head to the side, grinned with that huge mouth of his and she grinned right back at him. She wanted to hug him. He was so enchanting she reached out and touched his short hair without fear. "Bogie, you're amazing." She looked up at his owner and obviously caring friend. "He's incredible and I love his name. It fits him."

"Because of his big wide nose. He's named after Humphrey Bogart, the great actor with the big nose. My mom said Bogart was my grandmother's—who I never got to meet—favorite actor, so that's what I named him. Plus, my dad, before he died, loved golf and a bogey is a golf term. Dad dying is the reason Mom got me this amazing fella, so it all fits. Bogie has helped me through many hard times."

Her heart cinched tight. This dog was a beautiful bundle of muscle and love. "It fits then." The dog's deep black eyes continued to study her as she petted the rumples on his neck. "This is my first time seeing a Shar Pei."

"Shar Pei's are amazing. He's the best. Even at his age with all those muscles from running and flying through the air like he does, it keeps his muscles strong. So, he still looks like the champion breed he came from. The fact his tongue is both pink and black puts him out of the competition, which is how Mom was able to buy him for me. He was priced cheap, the breeder just needed him to have a home full of love. But you can look at him and tell if not for that spot on his tongue, he'd have been expensive and winning every championship there is out there." He bent over and rubbed Bogie's head. "I like his odd spot, makes him mine."

She loved it. "Sometimes something that seems bad is wonderful for the person that it is meant for."

"You're right. I'm Gil, Mom owns this place and

said we had a nice lady checking in. Said you're a motorcycle rider."

"Yes, and my cycle has a flat and Mr. Prudy is fixing it for me, so I'm staying here for the night."

"Thankfully," Max added. "Gil, she stopped to check out my prickly pear cactus and the tire went flat while she was there—better than a blowout while she was speeding down the road, don't you think?"

"I'm glad you're okay," Gil said, as Bogie placed his paw on her knee.

"I'm glad you stopped to see my cactus," Max added. "Because that's better than you being in a ditch on the side of the road."

She'd been ditched on the side of the road once, and was alone in this world but it struck her hard in that instant. She pushed it away but the thought of having blown a tire somewhere and not being found hit hard. No one ever knew where she was when she traveled. She was unattached and had made sure it stayed that way through life.

No one cared—the thought raged through her like boiling water.

As if sensing a change raging through her, Bogie shook his paw in her hand and drew her gaze to his dark eyes. Those eyes dug deep as if this fella could see she needed something.

Did she need something?

This sweet dog had Gil. It was apparent Gil loved Bogie and there was the love Gil showed toward the dad he'd lost and the mom who looked for ways to ease his pain by giving him this sweet dog.

What would it be like to be loved that way?

Her parents had left her on the side of the road, lost and forgotten. Then the question that sometimes tried to niggle its way into her thoughts made it there—what if leaving her behind was them thinking they were helping her? Protecting her from where she could have been with them?

It was an ache she always shoved away. Slammed the door—if they'd *cared* at all they could have left her on the doorstep of the church or a hospital, *not* on the side of the road.

She yanked her thoughts away from that time. "Lead the way." She stood up and forced a smile at Gil.

After picking up her belongings, she said, "I hear you have a talking parakeet."

Gil laughed. "That's Pepper, but he's a Cockatiel and you'll find out that he loves to talk."

She laughed and felt some relief. "Then I can't wait to meet him."

CHAPTER FIVE

Max was ready to head out but followed them inside the house. Instantly the rowdy cockatiel started singing as a welcome. Pepper loved to sing but no one ever knew exactly what he was going to sing. Today it was *Mule Hollow is the place to be…* Max almost laughed.

Pollyanna smiled as she met them. "That's his new song," she explained and looked at Lee Ann. "Pepper loves welcoming people into the place singing."

"What song is that?" Lee Ann asked, looking from him to Pollyanna.

Pollyanna waved her hand in the air. "Well, if you haven't heard it, then we'll start it out with Izzy, our new hairstylist. She came to town only because her two grandmothers, who lived to be, like, a hundred and something years old, before they had died, they'd asked her to come here someday. They followed Mule Hollow in the newspapers all the years from the day Molly Popp started writing articles about it after the Matchmakin' Posse started running ads.

"Izzy took care of them the last four years of their lives until both of the sweet ladies passed away. And the whole time Izzy was there, they talked about Mule Hollow. So, to give them what they wanted, she came here to work for what was supposed to be a short time. She wanted to give them their dream. And in her head and heart she kept hearing her grandmothers singing the old Television show *Green Acres* theme song that they'd adapted their own words too…adding Mule Hollow and some other lyrics full of dreams for Izzy.

When she arrived she kept hearing them singing the song in her head all the way from heaven. And, she found her man with them cheering her on."

"That's so sweet."

"And now we all know and hear Izzy's grandmas singing, *'Mule Hollow is the place to be. Love happens when it's meant to be. You'll find the one meant for you. Soon you'll know, da-da da-da. Soon you'll know, da-da da-da da-da. Which one's the one for you? Which one's the one for you?'* Pollyanna stopped singing, laughing too hard, as in the background, they could hear Pepper continuing the song over and over again.

Lee Ann turned and looked at the staircase, and sitting on top of the huge, winding staircase rail was the beautiful cockatiel singing its heart out.

"That's my bird." Gil waved his arm upward as if introducing the huge star of the show way up there, high above their heads.

Max's gaze went to Lee Ann, she was transfixed on the cockatiel. Her eyes shined—was that tears?

His heart thundered and he tore his eyes off her to look upward just as Pepper took flight. The beautiful green, almost neon bird soared downward through the air, following the winding stairwell with his wings spread wide. It was a sight to see. And then, Pepper flew right above Max's head before following the staircase back up to the top of the three-story inn.

Lee Ann's gaze locked onto his and there was

turmoil in those beautiful eyes that tore through him. What was her story?

It was time for him to leave. Why did this woman affect him like she did? "If you need anything, let me know. Prudy said as soon as he got your motorcycle fixed, he would haul it out here for you. But, if you need me to give you a ride to get it, just give me a call. If I don't see you before Monday morning, maybe you'll show up to pick prickly pears."

"I'll do that." She hitched her lip to one side, her eyes cleared as a half a grin appeared. He had a feeling that grin didn't go all the way to her heart because there was still a tenseness in her eyes. "And I am looking forward to learning how to pick prickly pears. Who knows? Maybe I'll get the hankering to start my own prickly pear cactus company and we can compete against each other."

"Compete, compete, compete," Pepper sang, drawing everybody to look up at the top of the banister and then he spun and flew to another area in the house, leaving them standing there not sure what to say.

"I'll leave you ladies and Gil on that note." And

then he headed for the exit.

He had to make his feet not run. And it took a lot to make his feet not run because there was something about Lee Ann Brown that dug deep.

What had made her look so sad?

* * *

The morning after arriving in Mule Hollow was Sunday, and Lee Ann had enjoyed her evening at the B&B. Now she was sitting on the patio thinking about last night when she'd gone outside to check out the surroundings. Gil had said goodbye earlier and headed back to college. He was young but had a good heart and she admired how much he loved his dog. It showed because he made special trips home from college at Texas A&M to check on Bogie. He was studying to become a veterinarian and obviously he would be great at it.

After he left yesterday, she'd sat in the wooden swing meant for two that was on the side of the B&B in a quiet, secluded area. Her mind full of everything that had happened since she'd stopped at the prickly pear farm, but the evening stillness and the fading light of the day, had eased her tension. The tension that was always a part of her life.

Thoughts of Max flashed into her mind. Her reactions to the handsome cowboy were totally different than her reactions to any other man she'd ever been around. She tried to fight them off, but the pounding of her heart and the memory of his gentle eyes digging deep into hers, as if seeing her internal struggles, won out as she'd sat there.

She didn't want to think of the cactus-growing cowboy, but no matter how hard she tried not to, Max remained in her thoughts.

It was troubling because she loved this place, was enjoying herself so thoughts of a man were not needed. Of course, it didn't matter what she didn't want to think about, her thoughts ignored her and continued straight to the handsome cowboy.

And the problem was she would be working with him on Monday.

Monday.

She rubbed her forehead as her thoughts collided on

the topic— She was stuck in between wanting it to get here fast and wanting it not to get here at all, and that was an odd predicament for her to be in.

Of all things it had her brain contemplating as it often did, wondering what her parents were doing now at the same time wishing she would never wonder about them again. Why were thoughts of Max making her think of her parents?

It was the oddest thing because she worked hard to knock them from her thoughts. But the question that often rolled around in her heart was if they ever regretted tossing her to the side of the road.

She tried to force the thought away, it was never welcome but it would creep into her thoughts… If she'd had her motorcycle, she'd have hopped on it and ridden for a while, the one place she got freedom from her past was when she was on her motorcycle. There, with the breeze encircling her and the world racing past as she aimed for somewhere down the winding road.

Her ride, her bike, her motorcycle, under any name, was her freedom. That two wheels of power was her way of escape. Roaming the countryside alone was the way she let go. Everything she owned was packed in the saddlebags of the motorcycle. She was a loner but did have a phone. It was on the lowest cost subscription because she simply had it for an emergency.

She didn't communicate with anybody after she drove out of the towns she'd stop at only for a short period of time to work. Keeping her small savings up to enable her to live the way she lived was a necessity. She met people but she never let herself make real connections because she didn't want them.

As an adult, she was in control and rejection was something she never wanted to endure again. Yes, in her head it sounded stupid, but in her heart that was just the way it was.

But last night as she'd sat there thinking of everyone in Mule Hollow, she wondered if as tough as she was, if she simply didn't have the guts to open up and let people in. If she didn't have the guts to stick around anywhere.

She reminded herself that making friends took away from her freedom, took away from her strength, so there she'd been last night, sitting on the swing taking in the peaceful evening. December in Texas had cooled off a little bit, but it wasn't uncomfortable, it wasn't freezing cold like up north where she'd been a few times. Nope. It was very pleasant; and she'd enjoyed the evening despite her displaced thoughts.

Today was Sunday. Her favorite day of the week. She enjoyed visiting churches as she traveled. She always arrived a tad late, hung out in the back then she left early, trying not to connect with anyone. Sitting there in the soft morning breeze, she remembered once she'd had a different experience. That sermon, it was as if the preacher was talking straight to her and it had hit home so she'd left straight after the prayer. But, the pastor caught up with her outside. She'd already gotten on her motorcycle and was about to crank it up when he waved her down and reached her.

"Are you alright?" he'd asked her, his gaze digging deep.

"I'm fine," she'd said.

He'd held her gaze, looked her straight in the eyes, and said, "Sometimes you have to let go. That's what God put on my heart this morning and it was meant for you."

She'd felt in her heart as he'd preached that it had been for her. But still, she wanted to get away. The message had been focused on a song titled *It Is Well With My Soul.* That song, the meaning behind it, had cut straight to her heart because it was written by a pastor who lost the children he loved on a sunken ship. As the preacher had preached the sermon then sang the song he'd somehow focused on her, staring straight at her. It had dug in deep and her heart had hurt.

She met his gaze. "I've tried to settle with my past and let it be well with my soul but it never goes away. But thank you." And then she'd ridden away and forced his words from her head and heart.

But last night and now, this morning, sitting here, her thoughts caught on the memory as she watched the sun rise on the horizon. The song played inside her, *It Is Well With My Soul*...this time the lyrics dug deeper and her heart ached. Her whole life she tried to make her past—her as an infant being tossed away—tried to let *it* be well with her soul. But she knew it wasn't.

The writer of the song had lost his children out in

the middle of the ocean when his wife and kids were crossing that huge open water to come be with him. But, their ship sank, his wife had survived but they'd lost their children. The strong but broken-hearted man had then ridden another ship out to where their boat had perished beneath those waters and he sang the song he'd written with them on his heart. The song for them and for God. He'd sung it straight from his heart, the poor man had lost his *kids* and he'd given it to the Lord.

She had lost her parents when they'd laid her by the road. As much as she tried to ignore it, tried with everything inside of her to let it be well with her soul…it wasn't.

Now, sitting there, frozen in place as the beautiful light of a new day rose, tears welled up in her eyes. Would she ever be free from the sting and pain of being tossed away?

She needed to be.

Wanted to be—

She yanked her mind off of those thoughts, slammed her feet to the ground and pushed the swing harder than she meant too and the wooden swing flew back and up into the air then down and up so she was almost flying. The air rushed around her, flowed over her and for the moment, Lee Ann felt as if she was flying free.

She sucked the air in and let that moment of freedom embrace her. Then she slammed her feet to the ground, planted them hard as everything washed over her, then she planted her elbows to her knees, leaned forward, clasped her hands, and she prayed.

She asked God to ease her heart, to let her have the courage to stay here in this town for a little while. To let the pressure of fearing connections ease up and let her enjoy it.

She knew she needed the Lord to keep her strong, keep her mind where it belonged and not to wander. Because she was happy. Sometimes as she traveled she was able to quietly help someone, but without real connection.

But still knowing she was able to help someone gave her satisfaction.

It didn't mean she had to stick around, didn't mean she couldn't be free…but right now she wanted to stick around here for just a little while.

Suddenly the familiar tune drifted down to her, drew her eyes up to the window a floor up from where she sat and there in his cage just inside the open window was Pepper and he was singing the title of the song and hit her hard… *It Is Well With My Soul.*

What? How did he know?

Her eyes were drawn to the beautiful bird, the singing cockatiel. Listening to the haunting tune, her heart thundered—those words sank deep like never before, oh so deep into her heart, and tears swelled in her eyes.

What was going on? She looked up at the sky, swiped tears away, needing something to help— suddenly the roar of the old engine signaled Prudy had arrived, saved the day.

She sprang to her feet. "Thank You, Lord," she gushed, then hurried to the edge of the house, rounded the corner as the wrecker pulled to a halt.

She had never been happier to see her motorcycle.

"Well, howdy," Prudy said with a wide, wrinkled grin. "I told you I'd get it back to you, and it's in good shape. And a *real* beauty too."

She grinned, it felt good. "I love that you love it. And it looks fantastic. You washed it." Her grin widened as his eyes twinkled.

"That's one thing I like to do when I haul a vehicle or a motorcycle back. I make it look better than it did when I picked it up, and I figured after you traveled all that way and gotten that flat after riding along Max's red dirt road viewing those prickly pears, this awesome bike really needed a wash to set it sparkling again."

"It definitely sparkles again. Prudy, you are amazing."

"Thanks, I try." He hooted with a loud laugh. "I been around a long time and been blessed to do what I love in a town I'll always call home. So I figure even if someone is just passing through, I can leave them with a smile by helping them out on their way."

"I get it," she said, staring at him and feeling a sudden similarity. "When I move around, passing through a place, I try to help someone when I can. Not that I help as many as you do but you do a wonderful job at your calling."

"That's the best compliment anyone can give me. I bet you do the same. I'll get your bike on the ground for you so you can ride it again. Are you staying?"

"For a short time. Not sure how long."

"I hope you come to church this morning?"

"I'll be there. I like to visit churches when I travel."

"I can guarantee you, you're going to get a warm welcome." While he had talked, he lowered her motorcycle to the ground, unhitched it, and then, he backed it off the lift. "Here you go. I'll see you there."

"Sounds good. Can you tell me what got my tire?"

"You got a nail in it somewhere but it held the air and lost slowly. *He* put you right where you were supposed to be." With that, he climbed into his truck, waved at her, and then backed out.

His words rang in her head, "*He put you right where you were supposed to be.*" Was her being in Mule Hollow God's timing?

If her tire had blown up instead of the air easing out slowly she could have been in an accident or somewhere else along the road. Timing was a hard and strange thing, but she realized that she was grateful that she was here. She was enjoying herself and ready to go to church today and see everyone.

That was an odd feeling for her. But she was also hoping she might meet *the* Lacy Brown Matlock. That woman had driven into this town in her ancient pink Cadillac and never left. Was that something one day somewhere she might be able to do? *Want to do?*

It seemed strange to even wonder such a thing but today she hoped was going to be a memorable day. One she could take on the road with her and smile when she thought of it. But that wasn't going to happen until after tomorrow.

Tomorrow she was going to ride out and pick prickly pears with Max.

She wasn't exactly sure what to think about that, but one thing she couldn't deny—the thought sent a prickly feeling through her that wasn't exactly like a sticker.

It was more like a tingle…a tingle of excitement.

CHAPTER SIX

Lee Ann rode into the parking lot of the church and parked her motorcycle. She'd just removed her helmet when two women walked up and introduced themselves.

Izzy Asher, previously Cranberry, before she married Luc, was *very* dynamic looking. She had long, kinky blonde hair and a big smile that instantly made Lee Ann smile too. She was standing beside a very similar-looking woman, but a little older. Lacy Brown Matlock.

The Lacy Brown Matlock. She too was a blonde but her hair was longer and wavy. From everything Lee Ann remembered people talking about, Lacy used to have wild and crazy curls that waved in the wind when she drove her famous, ancient pink Cadillac into town. Now, it was parked out in the parking area of the church and stood out like a bright pink flashing light bulb.

Lee Ann had noticed a soft metallic green convertible Thunderbird beside it. Lee Ann had read that Izzy bought her twenty-year-old T-bird because she'd come to Mule Hollow, had a wreck because of a bull and ended up wanting something that made people smile, kind of like Lacy's big Caddy did.

Now, here the two welcoming hairstylists stood wearing big smiles as they introduced themselves as she got off her motorcycle.

This was a great start to the day.

"You are the person we're here to see," Lacy declared, her smile dazzling. "God too, of course, but we knew you were coming today. And neither of us had had the pleasure of meeting you yet, so today here we are, the official *late* welcoming committee." She grinned hugely and her eyes exploded with warmth.

Izzy added with a smile too, "We know you already got a big wonderful welcome at Sam's yesterday and we're jealous, but we were doing hair at the salon. And like me and Lacy agreed, making someone smile makes our day." She grinned big.

Lee Ann liked her. Liked them both, but the younger woman was about her age and there was something about her that Lee Ann was drawn too. Her forward aggression in the big smiles and greetings. Wouldn't that be wonderful to be able to do?

The thought slammed into her like a gust of cold wind. She couldn't ever do that. Doing that meant putting herself out there.

And that was something she wasn't prone to do. Nope, she did things more behind the scenes and that wasn't often since she never stayed anywhere long. Now she held out her hand to Izzy. "I'm Lee Ann Brown," she said, taking Izzy's hand in hers and giving it a shake.

Then, she held her hand out to Lacy, who laughed as she stepped up, threw her arms around her shoulders and squeezed. "I love that last name. We are glad you're here and if you need anything, reach out to us and we'll help." She leaned back, still holding Lee Ann by the shoulders. "Who knows, we might be kin."

"It's nice to meet you both," she managed to get out. "I don't think we're related though, but I wouldn't mind if we were." She smiled inside despite knowing she was not a cousin or anything to Lacy Brown. Lacy was a *real* Brown, she was not. "Everybody's been really helpful. I got my motorcycle back from Prudy and he told me folks would be waiting on me this morning to welcome me. He seems to know a lot."

Lacy waved her long fingernails. "Prudy's been around a long time and he's a very quiet fella, but when you need him, he's there. And when it comes to picking stuff up off the side of the road, he's the one to call. So you did good." She cocked her head to the side, her blue eyes twinkled. "From what we hear, Max helped you out too."

"He's the one who called Prudy. I got distracted by Max's prickly pear cactus pasture and drove in to view it. For some strange reason, my motorcycle had a flat right then and there."

Izzy grinned widely, looked at Lacy, and then back at her. "Timing is everything as we all know. You heard my story maybe, but I came at the time that the Lord wanted me to and my grandmothers were singing up in heaven. It was their time and God's timing. It sounds crazy but it's true. I arrived at the right time."

"God's timing is perfect," Lacy said, grinning as she looked at Izzy. "He set you up and you know it. And," she looked at Lee Ann, "I think He set you up too."

Both the of hairstylists turned their gazes to her. She was stuck in the middle with both of them studying her intently.

"I don't know what to say. I'm here. I've read about this place for a long time and I…I was looking forward to coming to church this morning and seeing everybody. Prudy told me I would get a warm welcome and he was right. Now to be honest, I don't know what to say, y'all's minds might be going where it doesn't need to be going because just to be frank, I'm *not* here to meet a guy. Period. Yes, Max helped me with my motorcycle, got me into town and all that good stuff. But it stops there. Right there. I travel the country and have for the last five years. I just came here to see Mule Hollow because of all the stories I hear as I travel."

"Speaking of that," Lacy said. "You've been traveling the last five years. That means, from just looking at you, that you would have graduated high school and started traveling, right?"

Lee Ann was floored by her picking up on that. "Actually, yes. I started traveling right out of high school. But to be honest…" What was she doing? "I was in foster care my entire life so the truth is I started traveling the moment I was on my own. I worked until I was able to buy my motorcycle. And that took about a year." She didn't add sleeping in a shelter to save money so she could buy the motorcycle. "And now I'm on the road enjoying seeing the country."

Izzy cocked her head to the side. Her eyes deepened. "*On The Road Again,*" she sang the words to the title of that song.

What was it with this town and music? "Yes, I'll always be on the road again, and for always. I don't stay long. I come and I go, same as I'll be doing here. I'm just letting y'all know the truth. I come, I stay a few days or maybe a week or two, then I'm gone. I'm not here to be matched up. I *will* be moving along, and Max knows this too and is in total agreement. So, don't waste y'all's time looking at me." There she'd said it.

Lacy smiled brightly. "Don't worry, Lee Ann, we're not going to push you. We don't *ever* push. We're just here to give you support and direction if you ask for it. Just like Esther Mae, Norma Sue, and Adela. But I really hope you don't block things out because you never know when your life can change."

"I like my life," she said bluntly, then feeling bad for her aggression.

Lacy tapped her bright fingernails on her hip. "Great. I hear from Esther Mae that she's ridin' on your motorcycle this afternoon. And that she played *Bad, Bad Leroy Brown* for you at the diner. I also heard that she said, through your life you've lived up to that bad bad part, Lee Ann Brown."

The woman hadn't missed a beat. Izzy watched with a hint of a grin and Lee Ann pushed onward. "I can see news travels fast around here, and yes, I didn't lie when I said I can take care of myself. Anybody wants to pick on me while I'm traveling better look out. They might hurt me, but they're going to get hurt too. And that I can guarantee you."

Izzy's grin grew big. "I love it. How do you know you're so tough?"

"I took a lot of self-defense classes while I was waiting to get money to buy my motorcycle. I was top of the class all the time. And I had to use my defensive skills some along the way of my travels."

"You had to use what?" Esther Mae gushed as she hurried up to her side.

"Her fighting skills," Izzy said.

"Oh, I bet you got 'em." Esther Mae looked serious. "If your fighting skill is as good as your riding skills, then you're a gal to be watched out for." She grinned, big teeth shining. "*Now*, I got my helmet so you tell me when after church we're going to meet up. I'm ready to ride."

Norma Sue and Adela walked up beside her, both smiling. "Okay, so what's a good time for you? After lunch, we'll meet in town then we'll ride the long straight shot out of town then back. You'll see Mule Hollow on the horizon as we approach from a new perspective."

"Girlfriend, that is a very good idea. I love new perspectives. I'll see Mule Hollow rising on the horizon from the back of your motorcycle. How about two o'clock? The sun will be shining bright and our helmets will be sparkling for everyone to see in the sunlight as we come flying back to town. Thank goodness it's not the middle of the summer. You know, August and a hundred and six degrees, today will be a lovely seventy-nine degrees for our adventure."

Lee Ann liked this lady. "Yes, ma'am, we can manage that." But could she manage having this lady hanging onto her waist as they drove? Because she had never had *anybody* ride on her motorcycle with her.

She was a loner.

And that included her and her motorcycle.

But at the moment, she was up for the adventure. At least she hoped she was because no matter what, after church it was going to happen…she was taking Esther Mae Wilcox on a ride on the back of her red motorcycle.

And the thought—*at the moment*—made her smile.

CHAPTER SEVEN

Max stayed in the background as everybody surrounded Lee Ann. He didn't want her to think he was following her, and he wasn't, even though everyone else at church seemed to be.

As he watched, he knew she was being invited to have lunch after the service was over, and after that he was pretty sure that was when the anticipated motorcycle ride would go on. Watching her, he didn't think she was excited about the ride. He realized he'd gotten a little accustomed to her different facial expressions and though she tried not to, the tension between her eyebrows told him that her taking Esther Mae for a ride was a little bit of a problem.

Him wanting to step up and tell her she could

handle it was *his* big problem.

"Are you getting the same vibe I'm getting?" Clint Matlock asked as he stepped up beside him.

"I don't know, what vibe are you getting? I think she's worried about carrying Esther Mae on the back of that motorcycle. I'm starting to wonder if it might not be a good idea." He looked at Clint.

"I feel like something's not exactly right either, but I haven't been around her much."

"I don't take her as someone to risk doing something she doesn't think she can accomplish. I don't think she would chance taking Esther Mae on that motorcycle if she didn't know she could get her back safely.

Clint gave him a nod. "Sounds like you've gotten to know her a little bit."

"A little after our meeting in my cactus field and bringing her into Mule Hollow *and* eating lunch with her, surrounded by *everybody*." That was the truth.

Clint grinned. "Yep, you've been through a lot together in a short time."

"It's kind of like I'm out in the galaxy of the

unknown or something. You know what I mean?"

Clint laughed. He was around forty, nice as he'd always been and one strong cowboy. He still held the rodeos at his ranch and competed. He still helped anybody that needed help, and he still stood like a powerhouse for anyone in need in any way. Anything that needed to be done, Clint led the way. He was who Max looked up to, along with several other cowboys in town. But Clint held the lead alongside Lacy. If Clint thought the motorcycle ride needed to be stopped, he would step in.

"Clint, I always like the way you can take charge, but I really believe she's going to be okay."

"That's what I'm thinking."

"Something's bothering her though. You know she doesn't live anywhere more than a short few days. She travels endlessly and I don't know, I think it's the town that scares her."

"The town? Our town. Mule Hollow?"

Three questions. "Yeah." He hitched a grin. "I've been thinking about it. I could see her in church across the aisle from where I was sitting, and I had a great view—I mean, something troubles her. Something she doesn't talk about. When we were singing, *When We All Get To Heaven* she had a look on her face. I really can't explain it, but it's like the song really affected her. Oh, she threw it off. You'd never know it now, but if I hadn't been looking when that song was playing, I would've never known it."

"Songs in this town have an effect on people," Clint offered.

"I know it. Believe me. It's kind of like this town is built on music; fun music, sad music, jukebox music, radio, and angels singing too." He smiled. Thinking about Izzy and her grams. "I kind of have a feeling the grams were up in heaven right now having a good time watching and wondering what's fixin' to happen too."

Clint rubbed his jaw. "They're going to enjoy watching Esther Mae get on the back of that motorcycle. I'm going to enjoy it too." Clint's grin grew. "I know Lacy and the kids are ready to root for her. Anyway, we better get in there and help get everything set up, but believe me, it's going to be a fun afternoon. Just watching her, she's confident, like my Lacy. I think, like

Lacy, if she wanted something she worked hard and got it." He hitched a brow. "I'm just thankful in the end Lacy Brown wanted me. One day maybe you'll be so lucky. So anyway, let's go get that meal ready and help everybody sit down and then we're going to watch a wild and romping motorcycle ride."

Max grinned. What a way to put things into perspective. Then he followed Clint toward the fellowship hall, leaving everybody standing back there talking to Lee Ann. He sure hoped everything was going to be okay because he still felt something was off.

When he reached the kitchen, his friends, Jake and Cassie, who had helped him adjust to his new town the moment he'd first stepped from the van as a kid on his first day in Mule Hollow, were in there. Now, they were married and were always in the kitchen, saying that was part of their calling. They loved helping set up lunch after church and they were good at it too.

Cassie smiled, hurried around the table and gave him a big hug the moment she saw him. "Hey, we were watching from the back of the church where we sit so we can get to the kitchen before everybody else as you know—and to enjoy watching App and Stanley greet people. You know how entertaining those two can be sometimes. But today they and everybody else were watching you. And from where they were and we were it was clear that you were *intently* watching our new church member. So, spill the beans and tell us what's going on?"

He'd been so caught up in his thoughts he hadn't thought about being watched. Now it was too late. "There's nothing going on."

Jake grinned at him from the other side of the table. "You sure about that? I'm telling you, the Posse now has their eyes locked on you."

"They were sitting up front—"

"Applegate and Stanley weren't." Cassie's grin grew. "We've known this was coming one day and now you, our friend, are in the hot spot."

Their words slammed into him like a pan of hot grease. "I don't want to be—"

That just made their grins grow wider. Jake nodded toward the food tables. "Come on, they're coming in and we have to get everything set up."

"Wait, stop looking at me like that. Nothing is going on. I've got a business to get going. I got prickly pear cactus to harvest and jelly to make. And then I got to sell it. That's what I'm concentrating on."

Cassie and Jake just looked at each other, smiled and then went back to getting everything ready. He sighed, he hadn't convinced them of anything.

Not one thing. And if App and Stanley saw what they said, then yep, the Posse was going to latch onto him too.

Now what?

* * *

"Hi, Lee Ann, I'm Dottie Cannon. I wanted to welcome you to town. I heard you were out at Max's checking out his cactus and had a flat. I'm so sorry. But we're glad it happened around here and not somewhere stranding you along the road."

Lee Ann had been greeted by many but she instantly recognized Dottie's name. "I'm glad too. You are the one who married the sheriff and started the shelter."

Dottie smiled. "That's me. God blessed me in so many ways. I just wanted to welcome you and I feel the need to tell you being stuck here is much better than anywhere else it could have happened."

Something on her face struck a chord with Lee Ann. She felt a draw to the lady. "I'm glad to be here."

"We are glad to have you. And everybody is going to be lined up on the side of the street watching you and Esther Mae ride your motorcycle. We'll be cheering when y'all come back. She's been married forty-eight years and is ready to celebrate her friend Norma's fifty-year wedding anniversary next Saturday so she's not the one having the party but you'll help her celebrate hers with this motorcycle ride."

"Forty-eight and fifty years?"

"That's right, so we'll expect Esther Mae to be wildly happy when she rides back into town after her little adventure with you."

"I'll be *real* safe." She grinned. "Wow, those are a lot of years."

Dottie winked at her. "Love and marriage are

wonderful. I'm personally working my way to eight years and loving every minute. I don't want it to go by too fast. Have fun today." Then she turned and walked away, heading straight toward a very tall, handsome cowboy.

He plucked his hat off his head and gave Lee Ann a hand wave then with that same hand he swept it around Dottie's shoulders as she walked up to him and gave her a quick kiss.

So *that* was Sheriff Brady Cannon, the handsome cowboy who fell in love with the candy maker. Their story had been one she heard about too.

Lee Ann watched them smile at each other. It was evident they were deeply in love.

What would it feel like to be loved like that?

She shut that down like the slam of a trunk. Then she turned to head toward the exit door, but Applegate and Stanley were standing right behind her, grinning. "Whoa," she gasped, almost running into Applegate. "What are y'all doing?"

"Careful," Applegate grunted rather loudly. "We just don't want to miss it so we're stickin' close to you."

"Yup, that's right," Stanley agreed. "When y'all head to town for the ride to begin we want to follow y'all so we can watch you take Esther Mae on your motorcycle."

She stared from one man to the other. "I wouldn't stand there the whole time. Aren't y'all going to go eat lunch? Everyone will know when we head that way." The two guys looked at each other.

Applegate, the skinny fella, hitched a bushy brow at her. "Sure, but you got to promise us you ain't goin' to go on that ride without us being out here to watch. That'd mess up our whole day."

She couldn't help it, she laughed. These two just got to her. "Okay, I promise. No sneaking out. The ride will start in town, not here at church, but I'll wait not just for you two but obviously everybody wants to line up on the road and watch us ride away."

A very beautiful blonde-haired woman walked up smiling. She was holding the hand of a charming-looking cowboy. She placed her free arm around Applegate's shoulder. "Hi, I'm Haley Sutton and this dear man is my granddad, when he says he's going to do something, he's *going* to do it." She winked at Lee

Ann. "I'm just warning you. This hunk of a cowboy is my husband, Will. We want to welcome you too, plus warn you." Her grin spread wide when Applegate grunted.

"No need fer warn'n her," he almost shouted.

That got a laugh from everyone within hearing distance.

"Maybe not, Grampa. You need to turn your hearing aids up a few notches or not try so hard to appear you can't hear. Now, Lee Ann Brown, be as bad as you want to be but for certain don't let these two have you dropping your defensives with their hankering for fun." Those emerald eyes went from Applegate to Stanley.

Will grinned, his strong jaw hitching up with the grin. The man was strong, with thick sable-toned hair that just added to his look of strength. "Now come on, sweetheart, they didn't get you stuck in the hog pen out in the pasture. You did that all by yourself." Another roar of laughter erupted from his words, and then he added, "She's known to do a few things that she shouldn't do alone too. So, I'll just add, like I tell her, be careful out there."

Haley was smiling big. "He always says things like

that. And yes, I had a few exciting things happen in my life. And I still do, let's just say me walking across a rope, even a mere six inches off the floor, wouldn't be a good idea. I can be clumsy but I can also keep things straight. So, if I can do what I do selling real estate and enjoy life, then anyone can do it."

At her words Will tugged her into his arms. "Well, darlin' these days I don't have to worry about you running off and getting stuck in a hog pen or falling out of a barn loft. At least that's what I'm thinking."

Those emerald eyes danced as she looked at her husband with eyes that were clearly only for him. "You are thinking right." And then as if on que, they leaned together and kissed.

Lee Ann was feeling weak-kneed suddenly by the romance going on around her. And she knew in that instant that she was jealous. Not of them and their husbands but what they shared.

What would that be like?

These kisses were starting to really make Lee Ann's heart itch. Her *heart was itching*—her thoughts had lost it and that was for certain.

Who had an itchy heart? No, she was freaking out

over all this love she was seeing. And jealous.

That was where the itch was coming from.

And then she met Applegate's eyes that were glued on her, Stanley's too. Only then did she realize that these two dudes were reading everything she was thinking.

They grinned.

Goodness she was *not* in control so she needed a break. "Okay, guys, I'm going inside to get something eat." With that, she spun on her boot heels and headed through the open door—and straight into Max. They rammed each other, him coming out and her going in, bumped hard, and Max's hands grabbed her arms, tried to steady them as they stumbled his way, then her way, backward and out the door as he tried to keep her from falling but there was no stopping the fall. She was out of control and no help from the moment his hands had wrapped around her arms, pulled her close trying to protect her but her legs went completely limp! Her heart erupted and she simply melted as they fell—but he yanked her hard against him, twisted harder and took her on top of him as his back *slammed* onto the ground and not hers...

CHAPTER EIGHT

"Are you okay?" Max asked, looking at her as she lay on top of him, his heart beating rapidly against hers, his arms wrapped protectively around her, his expression a little strained.

The man had taken the fall and was asking how *she* was. They'd ended up on the grass since his midair twist had landed them in one quick splat onto the grass and not on the sidewalk.

"I'm fine, but how are you?" His gaze held hers, and then of all things, a slow, amazing smile spread across his face.

"I'm thankful this didn't happen in the middle of a pile of my prickly pears. Their stickers might be tiny but tough so believe me, this is much better than laying on top of all those little sticky pines."

Laughter erupted all around them. Her head shot up from where her lips had been too close to his and she found almost the entire congregation enjoying the show.

Shock filled her but did not override the fact that she was lying on top of this cowboy and could feel his heart thundering against hers. The pounding of their hearts together was far louder to her than all the clapping, laughing, and cheering going on.

She could barely breathe as she looked back down at the man who had spun the world basically to take the slam on the ground that could have been her. "Thank you for taking this hit," she said.

"Glad I could help."

She forced her response, "I think you and I have been the entertainment for the day, and we need to separate carefully, but still separate because we just got more rumors started."

Those amazing eyes of his twinkled. "Yes, we did, but we both know it's not going anywhere, so just let them have their fun. They're going to enjoy this and you're going to ease off of me. I'll help push you and then if I can stand it's going to be okay."

His words were gentle as he gave her a little easy push upward so that she automatically slid her legs off of him and sat on the ground beside him. He lifted up to a sitting position, their shoulders touching, he leaned his head over toward hers and whispered, "It's going to be okay. We both know what we want and that's all that matters. If we stay focused despite the rumors that we have basically erupted around us."

She lifted her almost limp hand, placed it on his thundering heart, met his eyes and forced words out. "We know what we want and I'm not going to try to fight this. They're just going to have to learn that we might be having some crazy incidents but *we* aren't meant to be."

* * *

Max was fighting back the way he responded to her. Letting her words sink in and hopefully setting him straight. Then Lee Ann yanked her hand off of his chest and to his amazement, she popped up onto her feet like she was a ninja, ready to fight. The woman was something.

She looked around while he looked up from where he sat, still amazed by the power this woman had as she gave the crowd a glare that eased up.

Then she grinned. "I hope y'all are enjoying the show because it's going to end soon, but there's more to come. Y'all all go on and eat, *then* I'm taking Mule Hollow's Daisy Duke—*Esther Mae Wilcox*—on a motorcycle ride. Y'all just might enjoy the show."

Her words were light and fun but he saw a grit in her eyes…a grit that said, *No matter what I'm thrown, I'm up for it on my own terms.* From his sitting position Max watched her spin on her boots and then those jeans and that pink shirt she had on sashayed with those hips of hers through the open door where they'd slammed into each other seconds before.

That black braid bopped from one shoulder to the other as if telling everybody watching—she had a mind of her own and nothing was going to stop Lee Ann Brown. And he believed it.

But no matter how he believed it, he couldn't get

those swaying hips—*braid*—out of his mind as he remained just sitting there on the ground totally upended.

* * *

The dining area was filling up quickly after she entered and Lee Ann wasn't sure where to sit. Her heart still raced, driving her into the room just to get away from the handsome cowboy who'd saved her in that fall.

Thankfully as she strode into the room full of tables and chairs her gaze was drawn to the side table full of food. It was loaded down with all kinds of food and standing at the end of it, a cowgirl with short brown hair and a big smile cutting a cake. She put the knife down and rounded the table.

"Hi, I'm Cassie, and I'm betting you're Lee Ann Brown." She held her hand out. "Are you bad?" Cassie chuckled as they shook hands.

Lee Ann laughed too and had fun with it. "Yes, very. I can beat up most anyone, good at what I do and so yes, I'm bad, really bad Lee Ann Brown."

Cassie threw her head back and laughed and squeezed her hand harder. "I love it. Oh, I love it. And welcome. And I don't believe you're bad. I think you're one smart cookie and I'm so glad you're here." She let go of her hand and looked over her shoulder toward the kitchen, and waved her arm at a cowboy who looked older than Max but younger than most of the Mule Hollow men. He grinned and strode their way.

He reached them and looped his arm around Cassie's shoulders. "Hi, I'm Jake, Cassie's husband. Welcome to Mule Hollow. Max is our friend and he was in a few minutes ago worried about you."

Worried?

"Yes," Cassie said as if hearing her internal question. "He's worried about all the matchmaking that's going to be going on. Thankfully, me and my man met the moment I reached town, but I had my eyes on the wrong man. A great man but not the one meant for me. The articles about sweet Bob got me here—he is amazing but I was mixed up and confused and needing this town to help me know who I was meant to be. And meant to be with. But anyway, we're glad you're here.

And despite what's probably happening to you, you'll be alright."

What was about to happen to her? "Nothing I don't want is going to happen to me."

They both smiled. "The Matchmakin' Posse has their eyes on you. Poor Max knows it, so he's on the lookout too, so no worries. We've got to get back to work but we're ready to watch a motorcycle ride today. So, I'll shut up now." With that they walked off arm in arm and Lee Ann just stood there.

This town was either odd or great, she just wasn't sure which one.

Standing there she heard her name called, and recognized Norma Sue Jenkins' voice. She turned and there stood the curly gray-headed cattle woman in her light blue overalls with a white blouse. A big wide grin stood out as she strode across the floor and the other two members of the Posse followed her. Esther Mae looked excited and sweet Adela was a complete contrast to her two friends with her perfect short hair that framed her thin face and enhanced those amazing sapphire eyes.

Kind. That was what Lee Ann thought when she

looked at Adela. Control was what she thought of looking at Norma Sue, and fun was what was written all over Esther Mae. These three went together like opposites attract and they were coming her way.

"Hey ladies, I'm in here."

"That was a great show you put on out there," Esther Mae said. "You're not hurt, are you?"

"That's what we came to check on," Adela added.

"I'm not hurt," she said softly. Touched that that was their first question.

"Great," Norma Sue said, grinning widely. "I'll be honest, we were worried about you but that cowboy did everything in his power to protect you. It was an amazing spin, like you two were on the ice doing a choreographed skating championship routine. I give you both a ten even if he did achieve his goal and he took the ground and saved you. That was a hard landing and so great to watch you both get up." Norma Sue hitched those brows of hers and grinned at Esther Mae, her expression was the same.

Lee Ann wanted to hear what she had to say, so she actually didn't interrupt. Now she added, "I'm thankful he did since it wasn't his fault I was running to get away from the crowd. And it just shows you that sometimes running is not the thing to do. And believe me, I know that. But anyway, I guess he's okay." She really wanted to know that he was okay. He had saved her from maybe falling on the concrete or on him lying on top of her and maybe hurting her. They were on that grass, but there was probably rocks and there was a flower bed next door. So yeah, they could have been hurt.

She hadn't even checked on him. The thought struck like lightning. Was she that bad?

Esther Mae waved her hand as if to halt Lee Ann's thoughts. "He's fine. He's not in yet because he's given you a moment to recuperate and he probably knows that we were going to get to you first."

Adela stepped up to her, laid a hand on her arm, gave a gentle squeeze. "Honey, sometimes you just have to relax. Quit running away. If you're only going to be here for a little while, enjoy yourself. And whether you want to admit it or not, we saw your eyes. You are attracted to that handsome cowboy."

How could they see that? And how could she deny

it when she knew all the way through her toughened body that it was true?

Lee Ann was stunned by her thoughts. Now looking at this beautiful woman who had a wonderful life and was just like a joyful walking light of happiness into the lives she touched—*at least that was the way Molly Popp portrayed her in her articles.*

To Lee Ann, meeting her and hearing what she was saying was like a punch in the gut. Was settling down and being this happy such a terrible thing?

"So," she forced the question out. "What do I do next?"

Esther Mae's eyes sparkled. "Come sit with us and have lunch and relax. What will be will be if you leave yourself open to possibilities.

Possibilities…was she open to them?

CHAPTER NINE

When lunch was over the entire church traveled to Main Street in Mule Hollow. Lee Ann hadn't completely expected such an interest. She was just taking a lady for a motorcycle ride. But Esther Mae stood there holding her sparkling rhinestone helmet and grinned like she was about to make a dream come true.

Lee Ann took it in and hoped she could give her what the sweet, kind woman wanted. She tried hard not to search the crowd and find Max, but her eyes didn't care and she knew exactly where he stood. Off the back of the crowd near the pink hair salon, his shoulder leaned against a column, his Stetson pulled low as if trying not to look. But he was and she met his gaze, then yanked hers away.

"Okay," she said, looking at Esther Mae and her gals who'd gathered close. "I'll get on first." That said, she threw her leg over the bike, standing steady on one leg and then steady on two. She held the handlebar and then without looking at anyone else, especially the guy who was on her mind, she looked at Esther Mae. "Can you throw your leg over the seat and hop on?" She doubted it and now wasn't sure what to say except to give the woman a chance to say yes or no.

Esther Mae wasn't a real tall person so it complicated everything but it was obvious by the determined look on her sweet face that she wasn't backing down. She stepped up and was about to give it a go when a very tall cowboy stepped up and grinned at Esther Mae.

"No worries, Esther Mae. I'm here to help."

"Bob, I should have known you would realize this short cookie couldn't get it done." She grinned widely, her eyes sparkling as much as the glistening helmet she wore.

"You know Molly is writing about this and she was the one who made sure I stepped out of the crowd to help." He pointed across the road and there stood a dark-headed, middle-aged woman with a smile. She waved, and Esther Mae blew her a kiss of thank you.

Lee Ann loved it. This town was as nice as Molly Popp portrayed it. Her heart tugged at the thought and her gaze almost went where it wasn't supposed to go but she stopped it before her eyes landed on Max. Instead she looked at the ladies smiling at their friend and wished for that too.

Then, Lacy's husband, Clint, stepped up and looked at her. "We've got this. Esther Mae, here we go. I'm taking one arm and Bob's got the other."

Then they did exactly that as Esther Mae just beamed as the cowboys each took one of her arms, grinned down at her and then they lifted her up in the air like she was a feather and had her sitting on the seat within seconds.

Lee Ann grinned. "Thanks, you two. Now, Esther Mae, put those feet of yours on those bars sticking out and we're ready to ride."

"I'm so excited. Thanks, fellas. Now, ladies," Esther Mae said to the grinning Norma Sue and Adela.

"Y'all step back and let us fly."

Norma Sue did the opposite. She stepped up and placed a hand on Lee Ann's. "Y'all have fun, but bring her back."

"I will. Esther Mae, hold on to my waist."

Esther Mae did exactly that, she grabbed Lee Ann like she was about to squeeze her into oblivion. "I wanna have the ride of my life, Lee Ann Brown. But I want to come back here to the man I love who is standing over there and lookin' *terrified*."

Lee Ann saw him, and he stood out because he was so terrified that she was going to hurt his wife. "You just hang on, and I'll get you back."

"Awesome," Esther Mae exclaimed excitedly. "Let's go, girlfriend," she gushed in a joy-filled voice and those tight holding hands squeezed the breath out of Lee Ann.

But, Lee Ann was ready and steady as she started the engine, revved it to the clapping and cheering, and then knowing from the grip on her waist that it was time she gassed the engine and off they went, slow and steady just like she wanted everybody to know. She was steady and nothing, nothing ever shook her up. This wonderful woman was safe riding on the back of Lee Ann's motorcycle.

"*Yeehaw*," Esther Mae yelled.

* * *

Watching from his spot, Max saw the redhead matchmaker grinning, her sparkling multicolored helmet moving as she scanned the crowd like she was looking for someone. She looked like she was straight out of a bag of marbles or rhinestones.

Max's brain shot to the old song, *Rhinestone Cowboy,* but Esther Mae was a Rhinestone Sweetheart. The woman had a heart of gold.

He'd grinned and looked at Lee Ann, she had a look on her face that said she might've been thinking about that song too. She was grinning from ear to ear. She was beautiful.

"If I like this ride as much as I think I'm going to, I'm going to buy my own motorcycle," Esther Mae yelled over the sound of the engine.

"Oh no, you won't," her husband, Hank, yelled back from where he stood surrounded by his older male friends. "I don't put my foot down often, and I didn't say no on this, but I will on you getting a motorcycle."

Esther Mae plopped a hand on her plump hip stared across the street at her husband. "Why, Hank, I could be mad, but oh how you love me." She beamed brighter than the rhinestones shining in the sunlight.

And Max didn't miss the startled look on Lee Ann's face as Esther Mae patted her on the shoulder. "That man cares for me. He doesn't want me having a wreck. So, I'm trusting you to get me back."

"Okay."

"But," she said loudly over the engine. "I also trust you to pretend we're in the NASCAR or something and let's go for a great ride."

Max almost laughed—this was going to be a show.

Lee Ann smiled. "I'm going to take you for a ride and you're going to enjoy it just like I did the first time I rode on the back of one. You'll get this sense of freedom. I mean freedom from everything once you get on this motorcycle. We're going to go down that road and you're not going to have anything to forget. You've got a great life out here. It's easy to tell and you have fun with it. Even though I was not real sure about taking you on this ride before, now I'm certain we're going to have a great time."

The smile that widened across her face made Max's heart stop.

The woman was a beauty, inside and out. His heart squeezed tight. What was it about this woman that caused all this crazy chaos inside him?

"Well, come on, boy," Applegate grunted in his ear. "You don't look at a lady like that without feelings. You know there's a connection."

"Yes, but confused by it—" Max then stopped, he'd said that out loud. He looked at Applegate.

The scrawny, wrinkled-faced man hitched one of his bushy brows up as he grinned. "I knew it. I knew it. But I can tell you, boy, you need to test those waters. Don't just walk away. Don't just close up even though you got plans. Plans can change."

He stared at the old cowboy and the roar of the motorcycle yanked his gaze back to Lee Ann as she and

Esther Mae rode down the street heading for some fun.

He watched them ride and he was jealous of Esther Mae. He wanted to take a ride with Lee Ann, wanted to get to know her better. Get her to trust him. Get her to let him in on the world he was pretty sure she rode that motorcycle to get away from.

And that thought stuck. He wanted to know what drove this kind-hearted woman to a life that included only her.

* * *

"I *love* it," Esther Mae yelled long and slow as they sped down the road with the wind embracing them.

Lee Ann grinned wide as she turned her head slightly and managed to say, despite being nearly squeezed in half by the happy woman's arms, "You get it, I love taking you for this ride. I didn't think I would, but we're going to have fun." She looked back at the road, focused because she wanted no wrong moves on this ride. "You're really going to like it on the way back, seeing the town rising on the horizon like it does all happy and welcoming."

Esther Mae whipped her head so quick trying to look over her shoulder that her jeweled helmet slammed into Lee Ann's red helmet. "Oops, sorry," Esther Mae hooted, laughing joyfully. "I think my head is spinning from slapping your helmet so hard. This is dangerous even when you're not falling off the back of this thing."

"Just hang on and we'll be okay, I promise." And she meant it. She leaned forward slightly, both hands tight on the handlebars and her knees actually gripped the motorcycle—there was no way she was goofing up this ride.

If something were to happen after she told them she had it handled and Esther Mae got hurt or worse, she would never live it down from them or from herself.

She wouldn't be able to handle the responsibility.

The fact was until now she'd never had to be responsible for anyone but herself. And in actuality, she had never taken anybody for a ride on this motorcycle, just her and her alone.

Esther Mae laughed again and something inside of Lee Ann felt joy. She looked over her shoulder and smiled. "I'm so glad you're enjoying the ride. Now, *please* hang on but ease up on your grip just a smidge so I can breathe and think straight."

Esther Mae laughed and eased her grip. "Now, breathe and drive safe because me and my buddies have plans. We're going to find you a husband. We want you here in town with us, setting down roots for the first time."

Shock filled her. "I don't want any roots. I don't need any roots. I love my life." The wind carried her decisive words as Esther Mae's arms squeezed tighter.

"Oh honey, you're just saying that when you know good and well God's got a plan and me and my gals are on the watch."

Lee Ann tried not to listen to the words. God had a plan for her, she truly believed it and she was doing it. As a kid who was thrown out on the side of the road she hadn't gotten run over. That was a blessing and she knew it.

She had been put into homes that had been safe and not abusive or bad and she'd been blessed with those decent homes. And yet she'd blocked everybody out.

She'd been determined to control her future and here she was riding free and easy on her motorcycle. Now, they topped one of those small hills and then there was another hill—then, a coyote came out of nowhere straight in front of them.

"Hold tight, Esther Mae," she yelped, gripped the handlebars for control as she had to yank hard trying to avoid the animal. The back tire held its grip as it slid slightly, and she angled the front tire to keep it from sliding out of control. The coyote let out a yelp and was out of their way, but she still had a fight on her hands.

She gripped the handlebars, held them steady as the new dip in the road hit them and they were at the wrong angle. They clipped a bump and then they were in the air…sailing as if parasailing, but Lee Ann knew they didn't have a sail or parachute to lighten the upcoming rough landing.

Esther Mae was hanging on like she was riding a wild bronc in a rodeo, but it wasn't a leather strap she was hanging on to or a saddle horn of a wild bull. It was Lee Ann's waist. Breathing hard, not just because of what they were going through, but because sweet Esther

Mae was suffocating her, she angled the front tire for the landing where the front tire would hit first. It wasn't exactly like keeping your vehicle from getting out of control if you hit a slippery water spot on the road and hydroplaned, but she was going to do her best. She held on, angled her body, which angled Esther Mae right along with her since she was hanging on so tight and in that split-second they touched ground.

"Yeehaw!" Esther Mae whooped once more as the back tire spun and Lee Ann tilted their bodies the other way to swing the wheel where she wanted it and hoped it followed through and then she gave it to the Lord.

Only He could get them out of this unharmed.

And by His mercy they stayed upright as that wheel behind them grabbed that ground, took on a grip, and they headed out on that road in a straight line.

Lee Ann breathed a breath as Esther Mae whistled and thanked the good Lord, again she released the grip on her waist, letting Lee Ann breathe once more. In her heart of hearts, she said, *Thank You,* that only God could hear.

She was thankful that she had not messed up, gotten

weak, lost her grip or her attention span as she had done what she'd practiced, been taught to do in an emergency situation. And they had stayed upright. Only God could have done that for her and she knew it. It was amazing.

"I cannot *believe* what we just did," Esther Mae squealed. "You, Lee Ann Brown, are just as tough as Leroy Brown. Only it was a crazy coyote that tried to take you and me out. You're bad, bad, Lee Ann Brown, and saved the day on this amazing motorbike. *And* you gave me the ride of my life."

Lee Ann wasn't exactly sure she could speak, but she wasn't going to let this lady know how shook up she was. "I practice what I do and I've been through a lot, but I'll just tell you, Esther Mae, that was a ride of a lifetime and you can thank the dear Lord that we're still upright and riding to the top of that hill before we turn around."

"I believe it and we didn't kill the coyote in the process." Esther Mae let out a laugh. "What a great day."

Lee Ann laughed and pulled the motorcycle to a halt on the top of the hill, took a breath as she put her boots on the ground and grinned at her riding partner.

"Esther Mae, I am an excellent rider, one tough cookie, but it came from being determined and giving it all I've got. However, I'll tell you right now, I gave that ride and that episode from that coyote, every ounce of determination and knowledge that I have been taught or experienced but you can give God the glory for us making it."

"Oh, honey, I did but He made you to be able to fulfill his plan, and girl, you did exactly that."

"Sometimes we get lucky and we make it, but right there, this moment that you and I are sitting here on top of this hill looking across there at that beautiful place in the distance with that pink building standing out. And we are standing here only because God held this bike upright. So don't give me the glory because I'm telling you it was God."

Esther Mae reached up and cupped her face. "Darlin', I'll give God the glory for a lot of things right now. Yes, He just saved our lives, but He sent you into my life and you, Lee Ann Brown, are giving me a joy ride that I didn't ever think I'd get. Ridin' on the back of a motorcycle, livin' through all that. If you hadn't come to town, my dream of ridin' a motorcycle wouldn't have come true." She dropped her hand and patted her arm again. "And that is how life works. We never know when God's going to use us to give somebody their dream or to give them something they don't know they want or need. And *that's* how the Matchmakin' Posse got our start."

Her words filled Lee Ann with something she'd never really thought about. "And He picked the right ladies for the job."

"We kind of volunteered because our town needed us. We thought we could do it alone when we put that ad out there. But God knew we needed Lacy Brown and he knew Lacy Brown needed us. And that's how that beautiful little town up there in the distance came about because it was God's plan. And I can tell you too, that's how He's been in everybody's life that He sends our way. And Lee Ann, He sent you my way."

Her big grin and bright eyes dug deep into Lee Ann. Did she need more than she wanted to admit that she needed?

She broke their gaze and looked to the horizon. She'd been several states away on her motorcycle ride and all along the way she had heard people talk about Mule Hollow, Texas, the place she'd never been. The place she knew like the back of her hand, she'd heard so much about it. The people she knew through word of mouth and Molly Popp's articles.

She had finally turned and headed back to Texas after she had read article upon article, but it was because she just wanted to see the town. It *wasn't* because she *needed* the town. And now, here she was sitting on a hill looking at that very town and feeling like she belonged there.

Heart thundering she turned her gaze back to Esther Mae, watching with those know-it-all eyes. "Now what she asked?"

"Darlin', it's seeping in now. I think you think God sent you here to give me a good time and I think He did. *But* I can guarantee you that me havin' a good time isn't the main reason for being in a town full of love and welcome. I couldn't have handled what you just handled. Anytime you want to take me for a ride, I'm ready. But I'm going to tell you, I see something in you and I know you've locked a lot of it out and maybe if you'll just relax a little bit, maybe out there in that prickly pear farm tomorrow with Max and all the people he's hired, maybe you'll enjoy yourself. Let this tension I see that's passing between the two of you take a day off. Then I hope you'll stick around for next weekend when Norma Sue and Roy Don celebrate their fifty-year wedding anniversary. We're going to party like it deserves to be celebrated, dancing and having fun."

"They've been married fifty years?"

"Yep and me and my Hank have been married forty-eight. So we'll be celebrating fifty not far away. But we're going to dance the night away next week, so stay. It'll be fun. If you want to ride out the next day then you can do it. But I wish you would commit to staying."

She wanted to stay.

That fact sent her world spinning. "Okay, I'll hang around until the party. Seeing all of you dancing will be a moment to remember."

"Fantastic. Now that that's settled, let's ride, baby

ride," Esther Mae hooted and Lee Ann smiled.

There was something about this woman that called to her. Something special that connected them like she'd never connected before—if she had a grandmother, this would be her.

The thought stuck her hard. Oh she had grandmothers out there somewhere that either knew she was there and didn't care or maybe, just maybe, they'd believed letting her go was the best thing for her. As she looked at the horizon, she let that thought take hold. If she could just focus on that then maybe things could be different.

Different. What about her life? Did she want to be different?

She wasn't sure but she did know they were riding back and this time it wasn't about speed it was about fun. Enjoying the ride and the person taking the trip with her.

A first for her.

She'd never had that person and like a rainbow calling to her, she knew this was something she'd never forget. "Esther Mae, it's time to ride and have fun. And

I want to thank you for giving me fun like I've never had before. We're going slower so no coyote dodging. Just enjoy the view and the ride like I do when I'm out on the countryside on my bike. There is just nothing like it. This time as you ride toward that colorful horizon, the wind blowing around you, encircling you like an embrace. Your eyes will focus on the spot—the *town* that's waiting for you."

She couldn't finish, she stopped talking when a tremble started for some crazy, strange, odd reason.

Then Esther Mae leaned her helmet-clad forehead to Lee Ann's helmet. "I am saying a prayer that you, wonderful, wonderful Lee Ann Brown, find your way to the place that waits for you like Mule Hollow waits for me." Then she lifted her head up and grinned. "All right, girlfriend, let's ride, baby ride."

Lee Ann's heart radiated with something unknown to her, something that pulled at her. And yes, they rode…

CHAPTER TEN

It was Monday morning and Max stood beside his red barn. It was the original old barn that had been here when he and his mom had moved onto this amazing farm.

Not long ago his mother and dad built them a place on the other side of the property. He'd remained in the original house right here among his prickly pears. He'd painted the old barn, added to it for the business but the front of the original old red barn was the same. New paint but that was it. That and the sign that said, Mule Hollow Prickly Pear Jelly Company.

Today this was where all of his temporary hires met ,and then he sent them out onto the large pastures full of the amazing cactus that produced the pear that he made his now-growing business on. He'd bought other acreage and now there was a huge amount of ripened fruit to pick and then for him to produce jelly from.

Several of the older boys from town were here, and some couples who enjoyed the process and the extra money for Christmas came from Mule Hollow and surrounding towns to join him for the few days the picking took.

He took care of the cactus and the ground surrounding them, making sure getting to the cactus was easy and no weeds to watch out for. Watching out for the stickers on the cactus was enough to have to avoid. He also didn't use the fire guns on anything other than the picked pears. Keeping the cactus as covered in stickers as God had made them. And as beautiful as they were supposed to be.

Everyone standing around for the official start of the picking held a basket, wore goggles, long sleeve shirts, a pair of leather gloves that left no skin exposed from the hands to the shirt cusps, leaving no room for the tiny irritating stickers to get where they were unwanted—in the skin where they could dig deep despite their tiny size.

Once picked, they'd bring their full baskets to him and him alone. The burning off the stickers was his job as was the making of the jelly he loved.

"So here we go," he called out and gave a grin. "The picking is now officially started. Have fun and be careful. We all know the prickly pear spikes come out eventually but they aren't fun in the least so keep covered up."

Everyone headed out to their predetermined areas and the harvesting began.

He watched them go, feeling disappointed because Lee Ann wasn't among them.

He had stuck around yesterday and joined in on the cheering as she and Esther Mae had rolled into town at a slow, easy ride, both of them grinning wider than Main Street. He hadn't taken his eyes off of Lee Ann.

He saw by her expression that she'd had a great time but when her gaze met his briefly he glimpsed something wasn't right.

Esther Mae gave her a huge hug after everybody helped her off the bike. And she told them how they had almost been run off the road by a crazy coyote, but Lee Ann had controlled that motorcycle like a pro.

"We flew over one hill and landed on the front tire then the back end twisted around and tried to put me in front of Lee Ann," Esther Mae squealed. "But this gal held control and forced that front tire to hit just right, putting me and the motorcycle where we were supposed to be. She landed that front wheel then the back wheel where it needed to be. Then, yeehaw, she yanked the handlebars like she was taming a bucking bull, and we stayed upright on that landing. It was amazing." The beaming of Esther Mae had caused an uproar of clapping and he'd watched Lee Ann blush.

The black-haired beauty, with the determined stern look had actually blushed a soft pink that had reached deep inside and twisted his heart one more time.

What, he wanted to know, was it about this standoff gal that did this to him?

Esther Mae had continued, pointing out that they'd probably been smeared on the road if it hadn't been for Lee Ann's amazing skills. Then everybody cheered and celebrated, and then Hank rushed across the road and swooped his wife into his arms and gave her a big old kiss. And to that the town went into an uproar of cheers.

He'd joined in as did his mom and dad, and he'd watched his father smile down at his mom and give her a gentle kiss that pushed hard at his heart. Love, it was an amazing thing to watch. Young, old, middle of the road, but he wasn't ready for it.

He was ready to burn stickers off of cactus and make sweet jelly that was putting him on the map. That was his priority. That and that alone.

Still, he'd watched Lee Ann until he'd had to turn away or mess up by going over and asking her what put that mixture of want and wariness in those beautiful eyes of hers.

Instead he'd watched Hank let go of his wife and sweep Lee Ann up in a lift into the air, grinning in gratitude before setting her back in her booted feet. "Thank you for keeping my lady safe." Then he gave Lee Ann a kiss on the cheek. "You being able to control that motorcycle in such a dangerous situation is remarkable. Now you've truly given Esther Mae the ride of her life, and for that I'm grateful."

The entire time Max watched Lee Ann taking the attention with calm, sweet eyes and he'd wanted to give her a hug.

Why was so much about her yanking at him?

And why wasn't she riding to the pasture, coming to pick prickly pears this morning?

The fact bothered him more than he wanted it to. Why did he want her here so bad?

It was ridiculous, so he turned and headed back toward the barn—then the rumble of her motorcycle came from the distance. He spun, his heart jumped like it was vaulting a twenty-foot wall, and he was thankful nobody was watching his reaction to the sound of Lee Ann Brown's motorcycle bringing her his way.

He was at the corner of the barn when she drove through the entrance and roared over that hill on her motorcycle. She was coming his way, making his day…and that was something he was going to have to figure out.

She rolled to a halt at the front of the barn, turned it off and then just like she'd done before she was off that bike in a split second. She removed her helmet and set it on the seat as that long black braid swung over her shoulder when she looked up at him.

"I'm here. Now what?"

He laughed at the words but the look on her face brought the fun. "You made it," he managed, his words sounding like he felt off-kilter.

"I did." She sighed, sounding a bit off-kilter too. "To be honest, I almost didn't make it at all. I got my bags loaded this morning and didn't even say goodbye to Pollyanna. I just hopped on my bike and headed the other way."

"Really." So she'd almost ridden off as she always did.

"But then I couldn't help myself. Esther Mae had told me yesterday that God brought me here for a reason. And that she wanted me to stay until Saturday and celebrate Norma Sue and Roy Don's wedding anniversary with y'all on Saturday night. They've been so good to me and well…against my gut feeling I told her I would. But, then I couldn't do it. I loaded up and headed out. But yesterday, the truth is yesterday I could have killed her."

"No, don't go that far."

"No, I could have. That coyote came out of nowhere. We were in a life-and-death situation. And like I told her, yes, I know control and how to ride, but Max, yesterday it was the hands of God that got my motorcycle back on the path. His will was what steadied those wheels as they landed back on that pavement. Me and Esther Mae wouldn't be here today if it hadn't been for Him."

He was stunned listening but more from looking at the serious eyes that said everything she said was the truth. "Still, you made it."

"Only by the grace of God or right now she and I would both be looking down from heaven watching y'all picking these pears. Actually, y'all would be getting ready for some funerals, or at least Esther Mae's funeral. Just the thought tears me up."

"No funeral today and from what Esther Mae declared it was because of you. Yes, God was involved but no matter what, y'all are here." His voice trembled with emotion. Her declaration ripped him up inside and he couldn't stand it as he looked into her eyes and saw the truth. She could have been dead.

Before he might stop himself, he stepped forward, wrapped his arms around Lee Ann and held her close. She was alive and she could have been dead. Just the thought of that ripped him up inside. She trembled in his arms, just stood there, not reaching to hold him, just stood with her arms by her side.

He couldn't help himself and hugged her tighter, his hand on her back, and it rubbed gently between her shoulders. He felt her heart pounding against his. "Lee Ann, I'm glad you're safe." She trembled again and his light embrace tightened. His heart raced as he looked at her. "I'm just comforting," he said, the words came out in a hushed whisper so he forced his voice to be stronger. "I hope you don't feel stressed or get on your motorcycle and ride away. I'm glad you're alive. I'm glad you're going to pick prickly pears with me today."

She didn't speak, just held his gaze, and then tears shimmered in her eyes. She closed them for a moment. "I am too." Her voice trembled.

"Are you alright?"

She nodded. "In all honesty, I haven't been hugged

in years, other than Esther Mae squeezing me to death yesterday." Her words carved into his heart.

She hadn't been hugged in years. "Why no hugs?" he asked, skipping the Esther Mae distraction. His arms tightened as realization rocked through him—he didn't want to let her go.

What was he thinking?

"I'm not one to get close to people, that's why." She said the words as she eased away from him. "It's me. I close myself off. But, thanks for that moment. I needed it."

He wanted her back in his arms. "Then I'm glad I was here for that moment. Lee Ann Brown, obviously you are bad in a good way." He smiled. "You saved the day and we're all glad, and I'm glad I gave you something that brightens those eyes of your up. Now, let's pick some prickly pears like you wanted to do."

"That is why I came. It's an experience I couldn't ride away from."

He was glad she'd come back…and again, he wasn't sure how she had such a strong draw on him but she did. However, he refocused on the most important thing and knew right now he was going to make sure she had some fun picking the fruit that was prickly on the outside but sweeter than anything on the inside.

For some reason he got the feeling that could also describe Lee Ann.

He got her all geared up with long-sleeved shirt, gloves, and glasses for protection and tried hard not to keep thinking about how empty his arms felt after she'd stepped away from them. But he was determined to give her an experience just like the first time he'd put those goggles on and picked pears. It had been like lighting a fire beneath him and it still was…only today, watching the joy that replaced the tears in this woman's face took the top spot on the best feeling ever list.

Once he'd shown her how to clip a prickly pear off the top of the cactus using her gloved hands, she was now grinning at him through her goggles and he was smiling too.

"It is as fun as you said it was," she said, holding the plump red ruby fruit in her gloved hand. "I can't wait to make jelly out of it."

Finally finding words he nodded, which wasn't

words at all. "I'll be starting to make jelly on Thursday if you want to come out and help."

She'd said she was staying for the Norma Sue's anniversary party so he wasn't asking her to stay, just have a new experience.

Never had he been impacted by a woman like this. It had always been easy to let go and walk away. He kept his heart to himself and always let go. Owning his own business and building an enterprise was his focus, not falling for a woman.

The ten-year-old boy he'd been riding into Mule Hollow in that van full of abused moms and kids had come a long way to today. But, looking into those amazing emerald eyes sparkling like gems in the sunlight drilled into his heart. For the first time those eyes had no worries in them, had no fear of the past and that joy took hold of him. Inspired him.

She looked from the pear to him. "If I were to take my hand out of this glove and touch it, even though it doesn't even look dangerous because those tiny bumps hide the danger. One touch of my finger and from everything I've learned, I would regret the touch."

"You definitely would regret it."

Her eyes went from him to the tiny bunch of invisible stickers. "That sounds like life in some ways, doesn't it?" They stared at each other.

His thoughts went to thoughts he'd never gone to before…if he touched her, kissed her like he had the sudden urge to do, he would be forever changed.

He would be opening his heart to the prospect of hurt, something he never planned to do.

"You are at a loss for words," Lee Ann said, dropping her gloved hand holding the pear to swing next to her thigh.

Thankfully she hadn't rested her hand on that slim hip of hers, saving herself from getting the stickers stuck in her blue jeans that could later be rubbed off onto her hands and then rubbed into her face when she washed her face at night—whoa!

His brain was going crazy with thoughts of a woman he barely knew. But he didn't want her hurting herself. That was the reason—at least that was the way he justified his thoughts.

"You're thinking like I think. Me, I'm just trying

not to mess up. Prickly pears are like life, there is the good, the bad, and the ugly. So be careful with that gloved hand, don't lay it on your hip and get a sticker in your jeans and then wash your face with it tonight by accident. When it gets on your hands, that can happen." That caused a warm, glowing smile to spread across her face. Amazing.

"Well, thank you, cowboy." Her eyes twinkled. "I won't do that. Believe me. I'm trying to heed everything you've told me, but it is kind of hard not to totally love this." She lifted the ruby pear up. "Whenever I look at the prickly pear, the beauty stands out, not the stickers."

Unwillingly, he took a step forward knowing he couldn't touch her because he had gloves on too, which was a good thing. He didn't need to touch her, but he needed to be closer. "There's another story to picking a prickly pear. When they're left alone in the hot heat, they can dry up, drizzle up and become really ugly cactus. They've lost their glow and don't produce this jewel of preparing for the jam. That's how people can be, and I realized early on out here that God gives us choices and I fight for my choices every day. I could choose to be really angry about my past before I finally met my dad, who didn't even know I existed. Or be furious at my sweet mom, who never told me about my dad and kept me hidden from him. Instead she married a dude who beat her until she realized that she had to protect me and we ended up here in Mule Hollow. Exactly where we were supposed to be."

They stared at each other, something that was happening a lot.

"Anyway, life can be unpredictable, and believe me, I don't have the answers for everything, but I do know that I love me some prickly pears, and they've given me the opportunity to be the man that I want to be. The guy that brings sweetness everywhere my product goes." He grinned, unable to stop himself because it was true. He might not be able to give everybody anything they wanted, but he knew that if they ate his jelly they were going to smile. And just that thought made him smile and it made the beautiful woman in front of him smile too.

Once again, she teared up and that sent the churning inside of his body into craziness. Once more. *What?*

"Max, I've never been around anyone with an outlook like yours. And the tears in my eyes are not my way."

"And I've never been around anyone with an outlook like yours, Lee Ann Brown. Bad, bad, Lee Ann Brown, always protect yourself. Always. Tears sometimes help ease the pain."

* * *

Lee Ann stared at the handsome cowboy whose words touched deep, deeper than she had suspected anything could ever touch her closed-up heart. "Do you constantly teach people about the good things in life and the way to look at things?

He laughed. It rang through her like chimes at Christmas. And Christmas was coming and as always she had the plan of being on the road when it happened. Of being nowhere near anyone that could bring more to it than she wanted.

Christmas was her alone time. Her time to thank the good Lord for helping her survive and for helping her be able to live a solitary life with contentment.

But now looking at this cowboy, this prickly pear picker, this handsome man whose eyes sparkled like a man who had something in his life she wanted, unnerved her. She didn't understand because he was putting things off just like she was, so it was confusing.

She managed to smile. "I think we need to let go of this subject and get back to picking these prickly pears if we're going to make jelly on Thursday," she said.

"You're right. We need to make sure we have plenty to do it with," he agreed, the smile hinting at the edge of his lips.

"Is everyone that's out there picking going to help make the jelly?"

"No, that's a family process. My mom used to help me and it's my grandmother's recipe. My grandmother I never met. So, jelly-making is now just me. My mom taught me but now she and my dad have added to our family. I have a four-year-old brother and a six-year-old sister. Mom spends a lot of time with them and the business is mine. She's loving her life raising my brother and sister and making my dad smile—which is always. He missed out on my early years but he and I have made up time since they reunited. And I'm proud to call Zane Cantrell, Dad. But—"

"But what?" she asked when he suddenly stopped talking. She'd liked what he was saying about his family, he'd found his dad when he'd thought he hadn't had one.

Not her. She knew she would never know her father but she loved Max's story.

"The truth is I've never invited anyone to help me make my jelly before. So, if you don't like it and want to leave and not come back, it won't hurt anything, just so you know."

He made his jelly alone, like her riding her motorcycle alone. Only he had a home, a place to belong. "Thanks for asking me," she said, and meant it. "I like learning new life experiences and I'm going to have fun like I am right now. So, we better get back to picking. What do you think?"

A slow smile came and his eyes held hers. "I think that's a great idea. So here we go." And they did just that.

CHAPTER ELEVEN

It had been a remarkable day. Lee Ann and Max had picked prickly pears one right after the other, no stickers allowed. Thank goodness for his gloves and long-sleeved shirt that he had given her.

When the rest of the crew came in about five o'clock, everybody was smiling and laughing too. They all gathered their baskets of treasure on the trailer sitting beside the barn. It was an amazing gathering of the ruby-toned pears and Lee Ann loved that she'd joined the group.

"You look startled," Max said, grinning at her.

She looked at this cowboy, this cactus grower, jelly maker, cowboy extraordinaire, and smiled. "Yes, what's not to smile about? Everyone enjoyed picking prickly pears. Me too." She fought off the way him looking at her made her feel.

There was no denying all the good qualities about this cowboy. After a lot of fun talk about the day they'd had all the workers headed home. That left her and Max standing there alone, surrounded by the picked pears and a beautiful sun settling on the horizon.

It was just a clear fact that she'd had a great day. She knew she and this cowboy could be friends, but friendship was something she didn't carry along with her as she rode out of each town she visited. So thinking about this as she stood there in the setting sun wasn't welcome.

"You're just going to stand there and stare at me?"

"No, sorry. I was just thinking what a great day it was. Now, I'll head out but I'll be back tomorrow and the next day too."

"Great. I'm hoping the pay is enough to give you what you need."

"Yes, it's plenty. I just work enough to help me pay for my room and my gas to get me from one place to the other. And I've got some stashed away for a rainy day.

I'm also a camper. There's a bedroll inside one of those duffels on my motorcycle. If I had to sleep on the side of the road, I would, could, and have."

Alarm crossed his face. "No way. You are not going to have to sleep on the side of the road."

"I didn't say I was. I just said if I never had enough and I needed to, I could. I'm not afraid."

His brows dipped. "Wait, you were riding out of town this morning and came back here to work. Does that mean you haven't rented a room at Pollyanna's place for tonight? It's the weekend so was she booked? And you're all packed up, aren't you?"

"Yes, that's the way I do when I'm leaving."

"You don't even tell people goodbye?"

"No—but I pay a day ahead so I never leave owing anything."

"You never connect in the places you travel?" His expression told her how he thought about her way of living.

"I don't connect. I move on when the time is right. That is just the way I live." The look on his face, in his eyes, told her he didn't get it. But that was okay, this was just between her and herself.

Then why, seeing the look in his eyes, did it bother her so much?

* * *

Max stared at Lee Ann, unable to wrap his thoughts around how disconnected she was from everything. Everyone.

"...I never leave owing anything..." Or taking anything with her she didn't want...like memories. Or regret.

He could never do that, he had too much to lose in those he loved and who loved him. Looking at her, his heart ached for her.

"I tell you what, if you're going to work for me, then room and board come with the job. At the back of that barn," he jerked his head to the barn door. "There's a room with a bed and a shower. It's in great shape, Mom made sure of it before she and Dad moved into their new home. And for a while after graduating I called it home, before they moved. I wanted my own place but didn't want to leave this place so it's comfortable. It's been empty for a while but it's clean. If it needs dusting, I can do it."

As if shocked by his words she just stood there staring.

"Take it."

"Are you sure?"

"Positive. It's just sitting there waiting on you."

"Then you've got a deal. I'll work hard, I promise. But I'm planning on leaving, like you said, after the party. Well, Sunday after church."

* * *

"It's yours as long as you want. And by the way, I live over there." He grinned and nodded toward his house. "I'll be cooking supper and it's included in your stay. Now, let me show you the room." He led the way through the barn and she walked beside him and shot him a smile…just what he needed. "I'll be at the pit with the fire going. Is steak okay with you?"

"Sure. Does the chef make them well done or is me

asking that an insult to your ability?"

He laughed. "No, ma'am, I can do a steak any way you like it." He raised an eyebrow. "Have you had a problem with that?"

"Once, the man burned it on purpose."

"I promise you come on over and we'll make sure that steak is done just the way you want it and deserve it after your hard work today."

She grinned. "I'm looking forward to your cooking, Boss. Me, I travel so cooking is not on my agenda. I'm a big peanut butter fan."

"Really?" He grinned.

"Really. It travels easy, it's protein and not much money. Add a piece of bread with it and it's amazing."

He stopped smiling. "So when you travel like you do, you don't always have money for food?"

"Not always, but I have to tell you, I really am a lover of peanut butter and bread. Now, if I had some of your prickly pear jelly stowed in my saddlebag to add to the mix with the peanut butter, it would be amazing."

"You'll have it. All you can carry. Really you live a simple life and love it."

It wasn't a question but a statement. She loved the way she lived and that suddenly was a strike to his equilibrium. She really needed no one. She lived and loved a simple life, a motorcycle, no attachments, and topped it off with peanut butter.

"All right, show me my room and I promise tomorrow after you've given me this room, and then you're going to fix me a steak. I will work extra hard while I'm here."

"Sounds good. Here it is." He turned the doorknob and pushed the door open. The room light came on with the flip of his finger and he was glad the room was here.

Glad he had a place to let Lee Ann stay.

Hand on the doorframe he stood there as she stepped up and looked inside. She was but a few inches away and his hand suddenly wanted to touch her hair, her shoulder and gently pull her close—"I'll see you soon," he nearly snapped, yanked his hand down, spun, and walked away.

It was time to cook and get his brain back on straight.

He knew if he made a wrong move he was toast.

And he wasn't ready to watch her ride away.

* * *

Max watched the steaks grilling on the pit. He'd moved Lee Ann's to the far side so it wouldn't burn but take its time so it would be well done and tender. His mom liked her steaks well done so he had practice in getting them like she enjoyed them, so he would see if he could do the same for Lee Ann. He wanted to make it as good as he could.

Standing there, he thought about the day, thought about the times when they'd been close, when he'd comforted her. Held her in his arms and felt so drawn to her that…he wanted to hold her again.

He wanted to hold her, kiss her.

Holding her in his arms and comforting her had felt right. Had felt like what was supposed to be, and yet there was the want to see if a shared kiss would be as great as his brain was imagining.

"It's beautiful out there."

Lee Ann's voice reached him and he turned with

kissing on his mind. She was beautiful and his gaze went first to those lips that he'd been thinking about. Then to those eyes and that look of soft but relaxed refinement.

"Beautiful," he said, talking about her, not the landscape. "I love—it. The land, I love the land."

She chuckled. "I thought so. You take amazing care of it."

"I try. I have all the prickly pear up to the ridge there." He pushed his arm back to point at the trees far across the pasture. "Then a deep ravine where the water streams through in a calm way and the animals love it. An eagle couple live somewhere along the way too. You'll see them fly over, often at this time of day." As he spoke the call of a coyote rang out. "Then it wouldn't be the country without the yelps and howls of the coyotes. It's a great place for all kinds of animals to live if they choose. This is a beautiful place for people to choose to live also, as you can see it was the place that I loved the day Mom and I moved in."

"I can tell. You look like the owner of the business. You're happy, tough, and make people smile because you love helping them."

Her words struck him in the heart. "You' re good, I do love helping people. I've been helped by a lot of people growing up, so giving back is what I like to do."

She smiled. "I meet a lot of people too and feel the same. I just try not to connect."

She had changed into a clean pair of jeans and a blue T-shirt, and he realized she had on a pair of sandals—black flip-flops. Her toenails were shining a soft pink tone. It was the first time he'd seen her toes and there was nothing about them that wasn't feminine. The woman might be tough, ride a motorcycle, wear a leather jacket, and take care of herself, but he knew she had a softness behind all that toughness. And the pretty, soft tone of her usually hidden toes spoke to him. "So you read people?"

"I try. Honestly, I don't hang around long enough to know if I'm right. My first impressions help me know who to seek out if I do need something. In the Mule Hollow case, the papers and all the people who read the articles helped me. But coming into town, it wasn't any of that that helped me find you—I mean meet you."

He liked her words. "You are something, that's for sure."

"You are too."

He needed this conversation to head another way or he might say something that ran her off or brought her closer to him. "Okay, I know you can take care of yourself but, tonight I'm cooking your steak just like you like it. I was just thinking, my mom, she likes her steaks well done."

He headed into the house, waving for her to follow and there he picked up the plate with the steaks on them. "Would you like something to drink, tea, water—"

"I'll grab a glass of water." She walked to the counter where he'd set his glass of water and set her glass of ice out earlier. "Thanks."

"You're welcome, the water is there." He nodded to the door of the refrigerator and she placed the glass in the spot and the glass filled up, and then she followed him back outside.

"It sounds from all you say that you have a good life, like you're living what you want."

"I am," he said. "Are you living the life you want?" Why had he asked her that question? Why had she asked him her question? Tension suddenly radiated between them.

"*Yes.* I told you I don't want to be attached and I live the way I want to live. I have no worries about anybody to hold me back. Unlike most people, I don't have to worry about any family. I'm unattached and I want to stay that way."

His hand went to his jaw and he rubbed it hard. This woman, it was driving him crazy. Yeah, he wanted to stay unattached, but it was because he had a dream of building a company. Not that he didn't *someday* want a wife and babies to enjoy life with, but why should her way of thinking strike him so hard?

Lee Ann Brown was striking him hard in ways he'd never felt before…was it in a bad way? Shoving the thoughts away, he worked on giving her a dinner she'd enjoy and changing the conversation away from him wondering if he wanted to try and give Lee Ann a different way of looking at life.

For him, this was a startling but enchanting thought. This woman drew him like no other ever had. And in the shortest time.

But could he really be feeling what his brain told him he was feeling? Could his heart really start caring for someone so quickly?

CHAPTER TWELVE

The sun was setting. They were sitting on the porch at the table. She had just had an amazing steak and a sweet potato with butter. She'd enjoyed his company after forcing herself to stop being tense.

She realized she wanted to enjoy the moments sitting there on the porch with him. She wanted something to remember because end of next week she was riding away. He knew it and she knew it, and it was as if they ate and talked. Her telling him about her travels, about driving all the way to the Grand Canyon on her motorcycling, riding around it and seeing the spectacular views. And then after seeing the Grand Canyon, she had taken a trip. It was a long trip through the flatlands and she made it to Yosemite.

That had been beautiful and amazing too, riding through the curving roads through the woods and the winding road that passed huge forest and stopping along the way to view the beauty of the sky and the valleys down below the mountain.

"It sounded beautiful," he said, then told her how he'd been traveling lately, expanding his market. He'd traveled mostly across Texas, but he had really enjoyed the little town called Dew Drop and meeting the great people who lived there. The Spotted Cow Café had been his reason for going since the owner, Miss Jo, had been one of his best customers. She was also a great supporter of the Sunrise Ranch for orphan boys.

"That town and ranch sound wonderful. I might have to take a ride there next. Try some of your jelly at the Spotted Cow Café." She smiled. "I love that name."

"It's an awesome place," he'd said and smiled. "They'd enjoy seeing you ride into town on your motorcycle."

She laughed and so their night had gone, fun, enjoyable, and a great memory to carry away with her. That last part she had to keep tacking onto her thoughts because she *was* leaving on Sunday.

But first, she would make it through the rest of the week picking prickly pears then making jelly with Max.

* * *

The day after giving Lee Ann a room in the barn Wes heated up breakfast then walked out onto the porch, to take Lee Ann a cheese, sausage biscuit and some coffee before they went to work. He crossed the yard and found her coming out into the barn area.

"Breakfast is ready," he said holding the cup and bag up.

"Thank you, but you didn't have to do that." She was surprised to see him as she walked out into the barn before he made it to her door.

"You're helping me pick prickly pears again today so I need to make sure you're feed and ready," he grinned hoping for a smile. He got it and it made his pulse increase instantly.

They'd wasted no time to get started as the others arrived and all took their places. Wes enjoyed seeing how Lee Ann worked. The woman was straight forward and did exactly what she'd learned the day before and she did it well. Needless to say it was a productive day. And at the end of the day he found himself enjoying the fact she was joining him again for dinner.

Wednesday morning started with rain, making it not a good day for picking prickly pears but he was thinking about Lee Ann. He fixed fresh breakfast sandwiches, cheese, sausage and biscuits then, his thoughts on seeing her again, headed out the door onto the porch.

"Good morning."

He looked over to find Lee Ann sitting in a porch chair looking relaxed but ready to work in a rain jacket she had on over her clothes. He smiled. "Good morning to you. You should have knocked and I would have opened the door and let you inside out of the rain."

"It's fine out here on the porch. Besides, I ride my motorcycle through worse than this. I just came over to find out what the plan for the day is now that the rain storm has taken over."

"We don't work in it." He held out the bag he'd put

her breakfast inside for her. And then he held out a mug of coffee. "Wanted you to have breakfast."

"Thank you," she said, taking both from him very carefully, avoiding touching his fingers.

He crossed the porch putting a bit of distance between. He leaned on the railing and watched as she opened the bag. "It's the same as yesterday. I cook for a few days so it cuts down on my time in the kitchen."

"You're a batch cooker." She grinned. "If I cooked that's what I'd do."

He liked her humor. "I guess I am. I cook three times a week and cook a batch of breakfast, a batch of lunch, and a batch of supper. Plus, I eat at Sam's often."

"Sounds like a good plan to me. No wasted time."

"Exactly."

"Yesterday was great so I'm going to enjoy this too. What's on the work of the day, Boss? Or am I supposed to walk back to the barn sit on the haystack and watch the rain from the end of the barn looks out toward the gully."

He grinned. "It'll be too wet so everybody knows to come tomorrow and be prepared to work in the mud.

I'll get you some rubber boots so you don't have to wear your motorcycle boots in the mud. I've got to go to town to Pete's Feed and Seed for some supplies that he's ordered for me. If you want to go, you can ride with me. You might want to go over to Heavenly Inspirations and see the ladies. Or check out the candy store, they have amazing candy."

"I'd like to ride into town and check out the salon."

He moved to the door and opened it. "Come on through the house. The truck is in the carport so it will keep you out of the rain."

"Lead the way." She stood up and passed close to him as she entered the house, his insides hummed at her nearness. He hadn't gotten used to his reactions to her but he wasn't complaining.

They talked along the way about his love of his business and the town of Mule Hollow and she seemed to enjoy everything. Another reason to wonder why she never settled down. They pulled into town and he dropped Lee Ann off in front of Heavenly Inspirations then drove to Pete's Feed And Seed and parked. It was just a drizzle in town, not raining as hard as at his farm.

Pete was leaning against the doorway, watching him with a big grin on his face. "Mornin' looks like you have a pretty rider with you this morning."

"She's working for me. And we got rained out today."

"I figured you'd be in today when I saw the rain was going to happen, so I have your order ready and waiting. The ladies are all over there at Lacy's salon so it may be awhile. Today is the Posses day and you know how it is when Esther Mae. Norma, Sue, Adela, Lacy, and now Izzy are all in one room."

Max grinned. "Everyone knows when they're together things go on so that's why I asked Lee Ann if she wanted to come to town. I knew she'd get to hang out with the ladies even if she's not getting her hair done."

"That's the truth, others go over there just to hang out. All of them are in there so no telling what in the world is going on in there today.'

"I told her I'd be here and no rush because I'm going to go down to Sam's and play checkers with the guys for a few minutes."

Pete was studying him. "You've got a look I've not

seen before, young man. And I'm just going to warn you if I see it, App and Stanley will see that twinkle in your eyes too. They're into that matchmaking like the ladies are. So, if there's something brewing between you and Lee Ann they're all going to see it."

Max froze, just stood there as Pete headed into his store. He glanced over his shoulder toward Lacy's place and caught Norma Sue watching him through the window. The huge grin on the sweet, frizzy-headed lady's round face stood out like a spotlight. Pete was right, they knew something was brewing and he felt like he was in a pot of boiling water. And he'd just dropped Lee Ann off over there.

Now, he wasn't sure what to do. Then again, one thing he did know was Lee Ann knew how to take care of herself so, with a determined look he followed Pete inside and left Norma Sue smiling in the window.

* * *

"You're here," Esther Mae exclaimed as Lee Ann entered the door.

"I see you got a ride with Max," Norma Sue said

from where she stood looking out the window with a grin on her face.

"Well, it is raining and I didn't have anything to do." She stopped talking suddenly. What was she supposed to tell them? That she was staying at Max's place and working on his land. She knew the instant that thought came that this was a disaster.

Why hadn't she thought about this before she had accepted his offer of the room on his property when she knew these ladies had things on their minds that she wished they didn't have?

Lacy came over and nudged her with the elbow. "We already heard you're staying at Max's place. I did Pollyanna's hair this morning and she said that you had decided to leave, and then you decided you would help pick prickly pears and you had a place to stay."

"You're staying at a room in Max's barn," Esther Mae added, grinning from where she sat in the pedicure chair with her feet in a foot bath. Beside her Adela was getting her fingernails painted by Sheri the manicurist— she was smiling too.

"My Bob enjoyed helping Esther Mae get on the

back of your motorcycle Sunday."

Lee Ann loved the sparkle of tease in Sheri's eyes as she looked from her to the grinning Esther Mae. "He was great helping Esther Mae give me the ride of my life."

"It was the ride of my life," Esther Mae said. "Amazing is what it was."

Sherry chuckled. "We all enjoyed watching you two ride back into town with those big smiles on your faces. My sweet hubby is the best, kindest horse breaker in the world, and he is cool to watch with a horse but helping Esther Mae get the ride of her life filled him with joy. And that fills me with joy." Her expression softened. "When I rode into town in the passenger's seat of Lacy's Caddy, I wasn't interested in looking for love. But love found me in that cowboy. So, I can tell you when it happens, it happens, and there are no regrets on my side. It's amazing when you find the love of your life, even when you're not looking. And I can tell you're not looking. But believe me, these ladies are looking for you."

The whole room busted into laughter as Sheri's

words were striking her in the heart. Why were they all laughing but looking at her?

"Calm down, ladies. Lee Ann, we're not saying everyone has to have a love story. We're just letting you know that when it happens, it happens, and sometimes it comes when you least expect it."

The sweet lady's voice and those amazing blue eyes dug into Lee Ann. *Was something happening to her that she wasn't expecting? The question riveted through her like a prickly thorn, a gigantic prickly pear thorn.* "I'm so glad it is happening for everybody who wanted it or wasn't expecting it, but was happy that it happened them. Me, I'm just picking some prickly pears. And yes, I am at Max's in the little room at the back of his barn. He's paying me to help pick the prickly pears, then I'm going to learn how to make the jelly. On Saturday I'm coming to your anniversary party, Norma Sue, then on Sunday, I'm heading off to find out what waits for me next." They all stared, her gaze roamed the room. "What? Why are y'all looking at me like that?"

Esther Mae came over and patted her knee. "Honey, we're just here to tell you that maybe over the next few days, before you ride off to another new horizon that you think, just relax and enjoy yourself. Especially out there on that prickly pear farm working with Max. Just have fun. Let life happen."

Let life happen. She controlled her life. She didn't just let it happen. She rode in when she wanted to and she rode out when it was time. But right now, looking at Esther Mae, her words wouldn't go away.

"Okay, so now that we've said everything we need to say, you just relax. How about a haircut?" Lacy asked, swirling the hair chair around so that Lee Ann was looking at herself in the mirror along with everyone else in the salon. "I think that beautiful long black hair you keep in that braid, needs a little trimming at the bottom and I'll be happy do that for you."

Lee Ann smiled in relief. "Sure. It's been a while."

"Then come on over here to the shampoo bowl and let's do this."

Lee Ann sat down in the shampoo chair, then leaned back after Lacy placed a towel around her neck and shoulders. It had been a very, very long time since she'd been in a hair salon.

"Now lean on back and let's do this." She did as Lacy asked and settled back as Lacy looked down at her and smiled. "We'll do a trim or something new, think about it while I wash your hair." She turned the water on then taking the nozzle in her hands Lacy began wetting Lee Ann's thick hair with the warm water.

And Lee Ann relaxed instantly as the feeling of the water rushed over her head, and the smile on Lacy's face as she worked helped Lee Ann know she was in the hands of a professional, a lady who knew that the touch of her fingers rubbing that shampoo into her hair with a firm massage was the key to helping a person relax. A few minutes later, hair washed and scalp massaged, Lee Ann sat up as Lacy wrapped a towel around her hair. That had been the best shampoo, one of a very few she'd ever had, and Lee Ann was glad it had rained and she'd come to town. Then she saw the entire room of ladies watching her with knowing grins on their faces.

"Lacy can give a great shampoo, can't she?" Esther Mae was the first to say.

"Yes, no doubt about it," she agreed. It was true. She was relaxed and enjoying herself.

"I love what I do," Lacy said. "Now over to the chair we go."

She followed Lacy and sat in the chair, had a cape placed around her and was turned to face the room though looking in the mirror. Everyone was watching and she caught Izzy grinning big.

"Now, tell Lacy what you'd like done to that long hair of yours. It's all one length and an open canvas for the talent that's standing behind that chair."

Lacy's smile widened as her eyes met Izzy's in the mirror. "Thanks, partner. You're just as good."

"Thanks, but I love watching you work your magic. So go for it."

Lee Ann was fascinated as the two hair stylists exchanged words over her head of wet hair. She got the feeling they were talking about more than her hair but she didn't care. She was in a hair salon about to have her hair done by Lacy Brown Matlock, and she loved the idea.

"Would you like a trim or something new?" Lacy picked up her wide tooth comb and went to work combing her hair.

"Honestly, I've never thought about anything other than my one-length hair. It goes in a braid for my motorcycle helmet. Do you have any other ideas?" She was giving Lacy space to do what she did and a tingle of excitement at a change filled her as Lacy's smile widened.

"*Girlfriend.* I'm telling you, this beautiful black hair would be so lovely and surprising with a long layer in it. We can leave it the length of your shoulder blades instead of almost to your waist and put long layers in that would liven up that bit of natural wave I see hiding in the weight of the one length. You'll still be able to braid it but have a different look when you're not riding on the back of your motorcycle. And with that high cheek-boned face of yours, layers will look stunning."

The room burst into "Do it." "Sounds great, go for it." And many other encouraging comments. And unable to resist, Lee Ann smiled. "Go for it."

Lacy waved her sparkling fingernails. "This is going to be good. I'm just telling you that sometimes a new style is like a new look at life. You never know if you'll like it until you try it. So here we go, let's do this."

And with her words spinning in Lee Ann's mind Lacy went to work. And the entire salon went quiet as they watched Lacy Brown Matlock at work.

And Lee Ann Brown felt no fear because she knew she was in good hands. In more ways than one. Mule Hollow was sinking in hard so why not try a few new things?

CHAPTER THIRTEEN

Max was sitting at the table with Applegate and they were playing an intense game of checkers. Stanley and Sam were watching and everyone else in the diner was enjoying their meals. The diner wasn't crowded because it was mid-morning, giving Sam a small break.

Max was looking down at the checkerboard when he heard the door open and didn't look up. He was trying to make the right move—

"Goodness," Stanley said.

At the sound of Stanley's tone, Max looked over at the man, and he was staring along with Sam at the door behind him. He looked at Applegate, and the man's stern, grumpy-looking face was slack, his jaw had dropped, his eyes had gotten big, and his bushy brows were hiked up to his cowboy hat. Unable to stop himself, Max turned to see what got this reaction.

His heart stopped the moment he turned and there stood Lee Ann Brown. The amazing, remarkable, breathtaking Lee Ann Brown.

He didn't even hardly notice the crowd of women who had come in with her. And Lee Ann hadn't really moved since she walked in. She looked stunned too, but amazing.

Then Esther Mae came around her and headed his way, Norma Sue followed her, giving her a little push to get Lee Ann moving. The ladies were both grinning broadly.

"Don't y'all love Lee Ann's new style?" Esther Mae said as she reached them. "What do y'all think?"

Max couldn't turn away and he was afraid his expression might give away the reaction taking place inside of him. Lee Ann's black hair had been trimmed to her shoulder blades, the front edge hung in a layer below her jaw and feathered down like where it just kind of came in and cupped her jaw just a smidge as the rest of the hair flowed in wisps, soft flowing waves. It was beautiful, but she'd always been beautiful—but it wasn't her looks that drew him. It was her driven personality.

Her self-made ability to overcome anything. But that look right now, there was no denying and he couldn't look away. Her gaze had met his too and he saw the uncertainty there in her eyes.

That uncertainty forced him to find his voice. "It looks great, Lee Ann. I bet you can still pull it back and get that helmet on it too." He grinned hoping to pull a smile from her. He knew she was always thinking about that helmet of protection and that getaway motorcycle.

Her riding away slammed hard on his heart, clenched it, that he didn't want to see her ride away. The realization was like a gut punch.

"You look beautiful," Applegate boomed. "Don't put that hair in a ponytail anymore."

"Now, App," Norma Sue said. "She does look beautiful but she can do whatever she wants to do."

"Don't go getting all mad," App added. "You all know she's gonna catch the eyes of every single cowboy at Norma Sue and Roy Don's celebration. Lacy knows it too."

Stanley chuckled. "Yup, this is a Lacy Brown move and we see it. Every single cowboy is gonna line up for a dance with Lee Ann."

He saw Lee Ann's startled eyes shoot to Lacy, who was still standing by the doorway watching the show.

He knew there would be a whole lot of single cowboys there and it wasn't Lee Ann Lacy was watching—it was him. Those blue eyes of that matchmaking phenomenon were on him and no one else. Lacy grinned and her eyes twinkled—she'd set him up and he'd fallen hook, line, and sinker—or horses stampeding straight at him. He ripped his eyes away and found all three of the Posse looking at him too. In that instant he knew he didn't want Lee Ann dancing with anyone else and they knew it too.

But he had a business to build, prickly pear jelly to make and prepare to produce in larger quantities.

And he was going to be working with her for the next few days before the party. If she knew the thoughts he was having, she'd be more stunned and punched in the gut than he was at the moment.

"Thank y'all," Lee Ann said, her voice firm.

He could tell she was forcing it. He didn't know if that was good or bad.

"I let Lacy do what she wanted to do, and I like it. Actually, I never had my hair layered before, never had it curled either but it's lighter and feels great. *And* Lacy made sure it is long enough for me to be able to braid it."

"That sounds good," he managed, glad he sounded fairly normal and not stressed over the emotions raging through him.

Her gaze locked on his. "Yes, I'll be able to fly like the wind on my motorcycle when I ride away on Sunday."

She was forcing her words too he realized. Telling them she was going to be riding away. So, there they were, both set on what they wanted.

Clearing the way, letting everybody know that her and her motorcycle would be riding away and he would still be here getting his business booming.

But him, all he was thinking about was wanting to

run his fingers through that layered hair, wanting to pull her into his arms and ask her to dance at the party.

Just dance, not stay.

* * *

Thankfully the rain had stopped by the time they made it home in the quiet truck. She had looked out the window the whole time. She loved her hair, actually really loved her hair. She had been blown away by the change it had made to her. It had softened her face up. And Lee Ann had felt another softening when she'd walked in and Max had turned to see her. The startled look on Max's face sent her heart racing and her mouth went dry as he stared at her without saying anything.

Was he as stunned as she was? They'd made it through the ordeal at the diner but now she was in a dilemma. Did she *want* him to like her hair, like her? As he drove them toward his place, he was quiet and so was she. The tension in the cab of the truck radiated between them.

She couldn't say anything and obviously he

couldn't or didn't want to. What was clear, she was positive that they were both attracted to each other and were both treading on a dangerous track. Very dangerous.

Neither of them wanted to move on the feelings that sparked between them. But something about the meeting at Sam's had pushed them both.

She didn't want to feel what she was feeling, and he had told her he didn't. So if he was feeling anything near what she was feeling, they could be in trouble. And that was the trouble. She *wasn't* looking for an everlasting life, an everlasting cowboy. She knew everlasting was a dangerous thing to want, to dream about and she couldn't let that digging need she felt when she'd looked into his eyes in the diner take over. That need would make her vulnerable. And vulnerable was one place she would never, ever be now that she was an adult. As a baby, she was easily tossed to the side, but as an adult she was in control and that was never going to happen.

No man would ever throw her to the curb. Everlasting wasn't something she could wrap her thoughts around because she had never had it. Her fingers had been tapping on the truck door frame and now, thank goodness, the ranch came into view.

"I'm glad the rain stopped, but from looking at the ground, it's still probably too wet now to work." He was still looking straight ahead and she put her eyes back on the road not wanting to see the tension in his jawline.

"You can just drop me off at the barn and I'll go to my room and work on some stuff."

"Okay, but I know you already had lunch with the gals. I'll get some dinner ready—"

"No, just do it for you. I've got plans." She didn't but she was going for a ride. Maybe a long ride. He'd stopped the truck and she pushed open her door. "I'll see you at work in the morning."

He nodded. "See you then."

She stepped out, trying not to fling herself out the door. Then she closed it. Nodded. Turned and headed toward the barn. Her heart raged and she didn't actually make it to her room but for a couple of minutes. She got there, grabbed her hair and started braiding it. Then she slapped her helmet on, grabbed her leather jacket and went back outside to her motorcycle. Within seconds she was moving, riding into the wind and leaving her troubles behind.

It was her way…but she'd made promises. So, she was coming back. She had said she would and she would. But for now, she let the wind surround her and the tears fly away.

This was her way, to ride, baby ride, nothing holding her back. Nothing taking her freedom. But today as she rode her brain didn't shut down. It rolled with every hill she crossed and her heart thundered louder than the roar of her motor in the back of her brain.

And a crazy old song she'd heard on some stupid movie played across her thoughts, she wasn't in a Mustang and she wasn't Sally but she was ready to ride, baby ride. Those words to the upbeat crazy song *Mustang Sally*. Ride, Sally, ride played as every hill moved behind her and her gaze was on the next one. She wanted to keep on going like she always did but she'd made a promise. And she couldn't break it.

Later that day, after miles were between her and trouble she stopped in another town, filled up with gas, grabbed a sausage on a stick inside the little store and ate it sitting out on a little patio beside her motorcycle. She watched the sun start to set as she drank her bottle of water and tried to make all the crazy thoughts in her brain go away.

She didn't want attachment. She had never had an attachment. If it could hurt the baby she'd been, what could it do to her as an adult?

Her landing on the motorcycle with Esther Mae holding on slammed through her, as hard as the landing had felt when they had taken that flying leap through the air, she knew it had only been through the grace of God that they'd survived. So, there she was as a baby lying on the side of the road and she knew it was by His grace she'd lived this long. Now she was strong and refused to let wishes take her to weakness.

No way she could deal with that ever again. She stood up and tossed her leftovers in the trash, then pulled on her jacket, hopped on her motorcycle, and headed toward the sunset.

Tomorrow was Thursday and she would pick prickly pears, then make jelly and do the same on Friday then on Saturday she'd go to the anniversary party to celebrate fifty years of married bliss…that she'd never know herself. But for Norma Sue, she was committed and that was one thing she wouldn't do, let down on a commitment.

But she'd go to it and knew on Sunday morning she'd be riding back this way, heading to a new place, leaving behind every memory she was building in Mule Hollow.

CHAPTER FOURTEEN

Max heard her ride away on her motorcycle and unable to sit still he walked across to his jelly kitchen in the barn and went to work. It had been a while and was late. Yes, she was going to help tomorrow but he'd decided he could get started. In reality, he only needed to let her help a short while to make good on his promise to teach her how to make prickly pear jelly.

Beside burning the many tiny stickers off the pears could relieve some of the stress pricking at him right now. At least that's what he told himself.

Making jelly took preparation and he'd been doing it for so long and thoroughly enjoyed everything about the jelly making. But burning the plums was oddly his favorite part of the process and the longest, so he was getting started. He also knew he needed to spend as little time as possible in this room alone, standing close and being driven to the edge of falling off the cliff.

He remembered his first time and all the equipment his mom had bought him from Pete's Feed And Seed. What an experience that had been at the age of thirteen. He'd become driven the moment he burned the stickers off the first plum. It was as if he'd been burning away all the troubles he and his mom had faced along the way. And in reality, it was true. The moment they'd bought this prickly pear farm, their lives had changed. His dad had shown up and he'd seen what love could do in a family.

Love that had a wrong start then found its way…

His thoughts went to Lee Ann instantly. She'd never known that. Never see that a horrible start in her life could have a great ending. Yes, she'd chosen her way of keeping her life in control. But what if there was another way? A way to real happiness? Taking that chance of opening her heart meant taking the chance of living through pain and of being tossed in a different way. Could she do that? Or with her head and heart in chaos would she do what she always did get on her motorcycle and ride away.

With questions trampling around in his mind, he went to work. In his gloved hand he held one pear after the other and with the torch he burned and sizzled the stickers away. It was quick and unbeatable, and it left the pear ready for a new future, bringing sweetness and joy to anyone who tasted it.

He wanted that for Lee Ann.

So he picked up his pace and burned away, needing to stay busy and not let Lee Ann steal the evening away with thoughts of things he knew he would never have from her. Things he wasn't ready for anyway.

Over the next few hours he'd filled up several buckets with the stickerless pears. He didn't even know how long he had been out there doing it, but he had a huge amount done. Leaving a small amount for Lee Ann to do in the morning and then the jelly making would begin. He had honed that too. Using his grandmother's recipe, the grandmother he'd never met, but with his mom's help he carried on her recipe and planned that everyone would know the joy of the jelly legacy she'd left behind for him to carry on.

The thought slammed into him in that moment. He'd never known his grandma, but he knew everything there was about her because his mom had made sure he did. She had filled his life with stories of Grandma, the jelly cupcakes she liked to make. Yeah, his grandma had liked to cook and she'd cooked more than just prickly pear jelly. She'd cooked all kinds of jelly, and in his mind later on, he might go to that too. That prickly pear was the unusual one. The one people could enjoy sometimes for the first time, and it was not the easiest one to find. You didn't find it on the shelves in many stores, so that gave him opportunity.

But he hoped to change that. But that's not where his mind had gone. His mind was stuck on Grandma and his mom. All the stuff his sweet mom had done to give him a good life. And then when his dad found him, he had done the same. Lee Ann had none of that. His heart ached for her.

She'd been tossed out, hopefully laid on the side of the road, not tossed out and injured, but who would know? And then thank the dear Lord somebody had picked her up before she'd gotten run over or eaten by an animal or just laid there and died. What were they thinking to do something so hideous to a baby?

His heart hurt, ached like never before. No wonder she couldn't open up. So many pregnant young women hurt babies because they were too young to totally understand what they were doing when they left it behind. Kill the baby, even before it left its womb. Put it at the hospital's special area, or at the church maybe, something other than the side of the road.

His brain hurt thinking about it. No wonder beautiful Lee Ann Brown had learned to be bad, bad Lee Ann Brown, motorcycle riding, never-staying-long-enough-to-lose-her-heart-for-fear-of-being-tossed-again Lee Ann Brown…he stopped burning the prickly pear and rage overtook him. He had to lay the burned-up pear down before he threw it against the wall, he was so furious thinking about it.

Yes, the parents or mom only could have been young and distraught and hurting…she could have been abandoned and uncertain so he had to think about that too. Everything about the situation was bad. But it was

Lee Ann who had lived it.

Lee Ann who had closed herself off from letting anyone close.

It hit him that this was her way.

His heart raged with pain for Lee Ann, anger and more just hurting for her.

He was a jelly maker. He had had a wonderful life despite the troubles before they found Mule Hollow. His mom had worked really hard to make sure of that, and his dad hadn't even known he existed. His mom in her own mind was protecting him from something she feared he might not want because he didn't really know. But now he knew that both his parents loved him dearly and they loved each other too even after the hardships they'd shared before he'd been even thought about.

Sometimes the world gave you an odd beginning like his, but thankfully his life up to this date had a happy ending.

He wanted Lee Ann to have a happy ending. Yes, she loved her motorcycle. Loved going from one place to the other without connecting with anyone in a way that would hold her down or bind her heart to something she was afraid to lose.

Afraid to lose…that was it. She was never going to lose anything again. And she was making sure no one could connect to her heart. He heard the sound of the motorcycle roaring down the drive and knew he was in trouble, not just because she was about to walk in and find him in turmoil. No, the big deal was his raging thoughts—what if he couldn't hold it together. She might see inside his head and heart that he was in trouble because he knew in that moment that he, Max Cantrell had fallen for Lee Ann Brown.

Really bad for him because she was one tough cookie and determined. And though he had had plans to enlarge his business before anybody ever captured his heart, obviously that was no longer an option.

Because he was totally, *wholeheartedly* in love with the wonderful, heart-stopping Lee Ann Brown.

* * *

Lee Ann got off her bike, took her helmet off, then yanked the rubber band off the end of her braid and shook her hair out it flew in the breeze and fell around her shoulders and felt free. Her life was similar to that braid. Yeah. She had braided her life up just like she braided her hair up, no layers in it. Her life had one strict, straight-to-destination trip, and she let nothing get in the way.

Nothing. She turned and looked toward the entrance of the barn. Something seemed different as she walked inside and looked toward the door that led to the jelly-making room. The door was open and she smelled the scent of flames, of something burning, and hurried that way. She found Max standing there looking at the doorway with a deeply stunned look on his face.

His protection goggles he'd pushed to the top of his head and he wore one of the denim shirts and gloves. He was well protected from any stickers he might touch but the look in his eyes as he stared at her was baffling. But there was a connection in their gazes touching, and she was afraid of it.

"Was your ride good?" he asked, his words low.

"Yes. You decided to remove the stickers without me?" Wrong question. "I mean, if you don't need me—

"

"No, I need you."

His words trickled through her like a low-playing song...*I need you*. Her pulse quickened.

"I'm just getting an early start. We've still got pears to pick but these were ready so this will help on time." His eyes dug deep and he took his protective glasses off the top of his head and laid them on the counter, then he pulled his gloves off as he stepped toward her.

Her heart thundered, thundered like mad. She wanted to step toward him with everything in her soul. "Then I'm going to bed, but I'll be here in the morning. Goodnight, Max." Then not waiting for him to say anything or take another step, she spun and then fled to her room.

She made it through a sleepless night knowing she had to see him over the next few days and make it through more pear picking and then jelly-making with him.

But, before she made it out of her room, there was a knock on her door. She hesitated, then kicked herself in to action—she opened the door and met Max with a smile.

He beat her to words though. "I brought it to you today since we'll be over here working today."

"Thanks." She took the bag, making the mistake of letting their fingers touch—the slamming of her heart instantly declared that she should have done what she'd talked herself out of many times during the night—get on her motorcycle—her lifeline and ride, baby ride. *Away*—far away. But all she could do was hold herself steady and take the bag, then step outside into the barn with him. Then he held out the cup of coffee and she knew the last thing she needed to do was chance touching him again so she hurriedly opened the bag as she strode toward the room where they would work. That left him to carry her coffee and open the door as she pulled the bacon cheese biscuit from the bag.

"I'll watch you do this while I eat this breakfast that you didn't have to bring me. Then I'll burn some stickers off the pears." She wondered if burning the stickers off the pear would be like yanking the crazy thoughts out of her head. Hard to do.

He leaned against the counter and crossed his arms.

"No, you go ahead and enjoy it. We've got plenty of time."

And so she took a bite and told herself not to admire the relaxed masculine man in front of her leaning against the counter, watching her with eyes that twinkled as if he knew she was trying hard not to feel what he did to her when they were in a room together.

Then, thank the good Lord, he turned away and started getting everything ready for the sticker-burning fun. She almost laughed at the thought. But, yes she was looking forward to turning that flame on and burning those irritating stickers off that pretty burgundy-toned pear. Maybe, just maybe, it would give relief to the building pressure inside of her. But it didn't because as she finished and went over to stand beside him, determined to be tough, tough Lee Ann Brown, she was once again put in a tough spot when he handed her the burner, held her gloved hand with his not gloved hand and showed her exactly how to hold it. Not only that, he held her other hand, having to stand close as he held both her hands with his and helped her burn the stickers off the first pear.

Her heart thundered, her hands trembled, and she couldn't breathe as they worked. But the stickers were burned off and the pear was slick, but she was messed up. Really messed up because when he stepped away, giving her an encouraging smile and telling her she could do the next ones on her own.

She didn't want to do them on her own. She wanted him beside her, standing close—but thank goodness she couldn't speak.

Her voice was gone it was so dry, so all she could do was nod and go to work. Determination took over as she burned the pears and by the time she'd burned the tenth and last pear her nerves had calmed. Some.

Anything helped.

Anything was better than falling on the ground in front of him because her legs had gone limp beneath her.

She was still standing. And that was good.

* * *

He'd made it through the day so far with the woman he loved and hadn't let the truth out. The truth, he feared, would have her riding away and he knew it.

Thankfully they had jelly to make and so that was where he'd focused. They cut the now sticker-free red juicy pears into chunks and put them in the large mixers that he had and turned them into a massive pink creamy fruit, then added the sugar, lemon juice, and pectin into the mix.

"It looks delicious," Lee Ann said as it was mixing. They were standing close and he could feel her nearness and had to fight off wanting to be even closer.

By the afternoon after producing their first jelly he hitched a brow. "Time to do a real taste test," he said, shutting down his thoughts about the woman standing beside him. Now, he focused on sampling their first batch of jelly. He toasted two pieces of bread in the toaster then they buttered the bread and topped it off with their fresh, still warm jelly.

"Goodness, it's delicious," she said, then took another bite, briefly closed her eyes and enjoyed.

He loved her response and she caught him staring at her when she opened her eyes. "That's the response we need." He smiled for the first time since realizing he loved her.

"I can't even believe I helped make this so good. *You,* Max Cantrell, have a great talent. Unbelievable. Your jelly business is going to go a long way. Not just because you can make what your grandmother left you as a wonderful memory to have, but because you're dedicated to it. You know what you want and you're not stopping until you get it."

You know what you want and you're not stopping until you get it... Her words were about jelly, but they slammed into him like a tire running over his foot, like a stomp on the knee from an elephant. Stunned, he stared at her.

"Are you at a loss for words? Just because I think your jelly is so amazing?"

"I..." His words trailed off and he couldn't take his eyes off of her.

"Is something wrong?"

Focus. "I always thought I had my life figured out," he said, locking his gaze with those amazing eyes of hers. "Finding my own dream and my own plan and driven to make it what I know it can be. But, Lee Ann, now I know dreams can change. Sometimes things you thought were priority, take a step down."

Her gaze shifted away then back. "Only if you let them. You have to keep your eye on the target." She set her partial piece of toast back on the counter and stepped away.

He had one hip leaning against the counter and he was facing her, only a couple of inches separating him from her. Now, she had put several more inches between them and he wanted her close again. "Sometimes," he said, his tone low, "things in your life change unexpectedly and you are thrown a stumbling block. I was—"

Her expression flared to startled. "*No,* I don't want to know exactly what you're talking about. If it's what I think it is then you need to quit stumbling. Focus, Max, focus on your dream. Because I can tell you, you're going to do amazing. You've got this dream in your head, in your heart and you've got the talent to bring your grandmother's legacy to life. Your grandmother..." Her voice stumbled and it broke his heart. "I never knew my mother, my grandmothers or my grandfathers. My mom didn't want me or my dad if he even knew about me or my grandparents. I have no idea what I could carry on. And I've learned to live with it in my way. But you, Max, can take this wonderful jelly and you can make the world know what a gift of jelly-making your grandmother handed down to you. You don't need anything getting in the way of that. Nothing." Then she spun quickly and strode toward the door.

"Wait, where are you going?"

"I've got to go to town." She stumbled over her words, but then she was gone just like that, and he was standing in the middle of his jelly-making kitchen in his big red barn with nothing. All this wonderful jelly and heritage he'd worked so hard to build felt like nothing.

Nothing at all. As the sound of Lee Ann's motorcycle engine blasted to life.

CHAPTER FIFTEEN

Once again, Lee Ann was riding. Riding the back roads alone trying not to imagine what he'd been about to say when she'd interrupted him. And now she was on her motorcycle. Her escape. *This* was her life.

She didn't even look at the scenery around her. She just kept her eyes straight ahead and made sure she didn't run into anything that might run out in front of her. If she went to town someone might ask her what was going on and she wouldn't know what to say, just like she didn't know what to tell him.

She just had to make it until Norma Sue and Roy Don's celebration and then leave. She wasn't staying until Monday. If she was able to keep herself here through church on Sunday, she would but she wasn't committing to it to anyone.

She hadn't really thought which direction she was going as she'd road away from Max's place but now the country church came into view and she pulled into the driveway. She brought her motorcycle to a halt and turned it off and sat there and stared at the old church. It was in the country but kept up well, inviting and inspiring, and the peace that surrounded it helped calm her down.

She remembered sitting inside surrounded by people who knew who she was, and she hadn't gotten out early and left as she usually did. Instead, she had gone to lunch with everyone last week. And now, she knew it wouldn't happen again. She wouldn't let her guard down again.

Sitting there, her heart throbbing, she saw familiar sparkling sage green convertible coming her way. It wasn't a pink Cadillac, but Izzy's little Thunderbird that had to be about twenty years old. And there rode Izzy one hand on the steering when and one arm stretched out the open window with her fingers spread wide letting the wind blow through them.

She was enjoying that same feeling that Lee Ann got when she was riding her motorcycle, the feeling of freedom. The air blowing around her, nothing holding her back. Lee Ann just watched and then suddenly Izzy slammed on her brakes and waved. Then with the press of the gas pedal, that T-bird whizzed into the church parking lot and Izzy pulled up beside her, all grins.

"Hi," Lee Ann called out, not knowing what else to say.

"Hey, good to see you. I don't normally see anybody out here this time of the afternoon as I'm heading home." Her grin was wide as she looked up at Lee Ann from her low seat in the convertible. That radiant smile and her wild, windblown hair was a look of freedom that Lee Ann wished she had. Yes, she rode her motorcycle but she had a helmet on and a leather jacket for protection. Izzy had her hair free, a T-shirt and jeans, and a seatbelt for protection. Unlike Lee Ann, Izzy let her hair fly free in the wind as her Thunderbird roared down the road.

She knew she could ride her motorcycle without a helmet but she didn't. She hadn't controlled much in her life but on her motorcycle she was in control but unexpected things came out of nowhere like the day she'd had Esther Mae on her ride.

Now she realized she and Izzy were just staring at each other. Izzy grinned. "Something tells me you need to let your hair out of that braid and come for a ride in my T-bird. I'm grinning, but you're not so my thought is you need a ride and maybe someone to talk to. Come on, hop in this car with me and let's go for a ride."

Lee Ann wanted to but held back. "I—"

"Lacy taught me that riding in a vehicle with the top down and the wind blowing around you frees your mind and gives you time to think and feel. Probably just like on a motorcycle, but if you ride with me I'll concentrate on the road and you can relax. Come on, ride with me."

Lee Ann couldn't resist, she did need something and maybe Izzy was right. She hopped off her motorcycle, took off her helmet and set it on the bike, grabbed her keys out of the ignition, stuffed them in her jeans as she walked straight around ,opened the passenger door, and slid into the sea green tinted leather seat. "I love your car," she said as she closed the door.

"Thanks, so do I. It's not as flamboyant as Lacy's pink Cadillac, but there's nothing like the wind in your hair and face to wake you up and keep you alert as you enjoy the ride and beauty of what God has created. Before I took a ride in Lacy's Caddy, I never thought about it, but boy did I need it. And Lacy took me for a ride and showed me when I was at my worst. So, now I have my own ride and I love it. When I saw it sitting there I knew I wanted it. And now it's mine. So buckle up and let's go for a ride."

She did just that. And Izzy gave her a grin, then they drove from the parking lot onto the back roads of Mule Hollow, and down the road.

Just a few feet down the road Izzy grinned at her then punched her foot to the floor and the car took off. It shot from almost zero to sixty miles an hour in less than it seemed like three seconds.

"Whoa, this little car can really go." Her hand had gripped the top of the door but a grin flew across her face with the swirling wind that surrounded her.

This was what she'd needed. The turmoil inside her swirled and the breeze seemed to set her free. She looked at Izzy, who was grinning wide.

"It will fly but believe me, I only speed when needed." She slowed the car to a normal speed but the wind still set her free as it continued embracing her and blowing away her pain.

Pain?

"It'll go fast but just the feel of letting go is all we need."

"So, I hope you're not dangerous with it. I mean, it's kind of like a motorcycle. I can do a lot on mine, but I don't drive too dangerous. I don't feel like ending up on the side of the road." She'd been tossed there in the beginning and had no plans to throw herself on the side of the road.

Izzy waved her hand. "Same here, so don't worry, we are not going to die today. Not unless the Lord bursts our tires." She eased off the gas pedal. "It's just fun and a little extra breeze in your face and then just like this riding and relaxing. This is what I prefer. I just goosed it to give you a little thrill. But the real reason of putting your foot to the pedal is having speed when needed, the ability to move you out of the way of another car or truck or anything coming at you. That's the way I look at it."

The words drilled into Lee Ann. That's kind of how she felt on her motorcycle. She wasn't sure what would happen if she never had her motorcycle. She'd kept working part-time jobs to pay for the expenses of keeping it updated and pay for rooms when needed. And sometimes she did camp out on the side of a dark road all alone. She didn't always feel safe but it was her way of life. But now, as the wind blew across her, she knew there was one thing she felt when she was at the ranch with Max, and it was safe. He was in the house and she was in the barn, but all she'd had to do was give a holler and she knew he would be there. Looking out for her.

The thought stayed on her heart, and she started drumming her fingers on the top of the door where the window was down and the breeze helping her tap.

Izzy looked at her. "Drumming those fingers. You're thinking. What's got your mind rolling?"

"Why does life like to throw things at us sometimes?" She needed to talk and Izzy was the one who had come along.

Izzy, with one hand on the steering wheel, reached out with her other hand and patted Lee Ann's shoulder, then put her hand back on the steering wheel. "I found out that's just the way it is. My sweet grandmothers, my "Grammys" loved me dearly and when they needed me, I gave up my salon business and went to take care of them. I never knew that me doing that for them would be what would lead me to this crazy life I love here in Mule Hollow. Here with all the ladies at the salon but most of all finding and marrying the man of my dreams. Life is full of ups and downs and craziness that we sometimes can never imagine."

Lee Ann listened and stopped drumming her fingers on the car as Izzy let her free hand hang out the window, letting the breeze blow through her fingertips. Lee Ann did the same, letting the wind blow through them.

It felt wonderful. She stretched her fingers wide and it felt as if the wind drifted through her fingers, and odd as it was, it eased the pain inside of her.

She teared up. One thing about her motorcycle. She had a face mask and a windshield, but here she had a free hand for the wind to touch.

It hit her. "I wonder if letting go of your past and looking forward to tomorrow feels like the wind blowing through these fingers right now?"

"Now you're talking. It does. Are you feeling like letting your pain go like that wind blowing through your fingers right now?"

"Close." She kept her hand out there, but she took her other hand and she rubbed her forehead. She felt tears against her eyelids. "It's not something I know I can do."

Izzy slowed the T-bird down and they were inching along the road. "Now, I think you said you're coming to Norma Sue's anniversary party, right?"

"Yes. That's the only reason I'm still here. I made some promises and I plan to keep them."

"So what if you just relax, keep some fingers out there and think about letting everything flow through them and go away. Our past is our past and whatever happened to you must have been bad. I see it in your eyes. Can you let it go? Move forward, maybe put your feet down instead of riding away all the time."

Izzy's eyes drilled into her. "I don't know," Lee Ann whispered.

"You know my grams are why I came because they read every article Molly Popp wrote. But they were creative too and made up a song that goes with the old *Green Acres* show. And I hear them singing in my head right now—*Mule Hollow is the place to be. Love happens when it's meant to be. You'll find the one that's meant for you…only if you open up your heart…"*

Lee Ann grinned. Pepper's song, the cute little tune that went with it and the deep-hearted look Izzy gave her. "That's crazy how heart-touching that is. Your grams must have been fun."

"They were," Izzy laughed. "They're in heaven and still singing in my mind like they're right here beside me. Them singing that song and their love for me and Mule Hollow brought me here. I wasn't looking to stay or for love but that's what was waiting for me here. Not everyone is looking for love or wanting it, but I can tell anyone not to close your heart. I tell everybody, even if you hadn't found it now, don't close your heart because when the time is right, it happens."

"You had wonderful grandmas. All that stuff I never had, and that's kind of driving me crazy."

"No grandmothers?"

"No. None. I never quite worried about it or thought about it as much before. But, since I've been here it's as if everything in my life is slamming into me."

Izzy's eyes danced. "That's because just like I found out, and just like I said, Mule Hollow is the place to be. Even if you're not looking for a man to love you, this town is full of smart, wonderful, older ladies who will call you their own. And I am not the only one who says that. So, come on, I'll head back and take you to your motorcycle. I'll look forward to seeing you there. Hope I helped you relax a little. Also, don't ride your motorcycle to the celebration. I have a feeling there's a cowboy out there in that prickly pear patch who would give you a ride. You might have to ask him. But I think he'll probably dance with you a few times too."

Did she want him too?

"If you'll just relax and let life happen while you're here. You can leave your door open on leaving on Sunday. Open your heart a little bit. Love happens, and even if you don't let it, maybe you'll get a good taste of it and if you can't stay, maybe you'll come back. Whatever. Just give it a shot. Enjoy yourself at the party."

They got back to her motorcycle and she got out of the car. Izzy jumped to the ground and threw her small arms around Lee Ann. "Okay, girlfriend, I don't know if I helped you or not, but I tell you what, when I decided to live in Mule Hall, it's because I was going to do what the Lord sent me to do. And He put people in my path like he did for Lacy Brown. You just do what you feel is right for you. God laid this on my heart."

Lee Ann reached out and hugged Izzy again, "You helped me. I don't let people close, but Izzy, I think me and you could be friends."

Izzy grinned. "Girlfriend, we already are friends. You ride away if you want to, but always remember in Mule Hollow, you've got friends for life, not just me. You might never call me, but if you show back up, I'm here, Lord willing." She winked then headed back to her T-bird, and set her butt on the door, threw her legs over, and slid into that seat. "See you later, gator." Then she drove toward her home. And the man she loved.

Lee Ann took a deep breath, settled on her motorcycle, put her helmet on, and headed back to the prickly pear farm and the man who had her world spinning out of control.

She was going to take the advice of Izzy and try and relax. *Try* was the keyword.

CHAPTER SIXTEEN

When Max walked out onto his porch after his sleepless night, there sat Lee Ann on his porch. He'd heard her come back later that evening but he'd stayed away. Now seeing her took him by surprise.

"Good morning," she said, her voice low, calm as the morning breeze.

He had almost expected her not to come back last night after their conversation after she had turned and walked away, leaving him there with his mind completely off-kilter. He had expected that maybe she had ridden away this morning. Or in the middle of the night, since that's what she did.

"Good morning. I thought that I would just assure you that I'm here to work. I don't want to lead you on.

There's that thing that you and I both feel. And I wondered if we could finish making the jelly today, then I can at least say I actually helped with this season's jelly making. And really enjoyed it. *And* I mean that when I say it."

He had no words, at least for the moment, then she continued.

"Instead of going to town yesterday, I just rode. I ended up at the church, sitting out there in the parking lot. Seems like God always takes me to the church some way or the other. And while I was sitting there contemplating this dilemma that I find myself in, Izzy drove up in her cute little T-bird and took me on a ride. Have you ever held your hand out a window with your fingers spread wide and let the wind just blow through them?"

He couldn't find words as her words drilled though him like the breeze on her fingers. He finally found words. "I haven't done that but did you like it?"

"Actually, I did." A smile spread over her face. "I really did. It was as freeing as riding on my motorcycle but different. When I'm riding my motorcycle, I don't let go and hold my hand out with my fingers spread wide. I need two hands on the wheel." Her eyes sparkled. "I didn't realize the way that it feels is a lot like riding a motorcycle. It helps when you're stressed out. I really enjoyed the convertible. It helps when you're stressed out."

Unable to stop himself, he stepped toward her, his heart pounding. "I didn't mean to stress you out yesterday," he offered. He'd done this and he knew it. It was a miracle that she was still here.

"It's not you. It's my world that has brought all the pressure on." She stood up. "I mean, we have prickly pear jelly to make—I don't mean to take up the conversation."

"The jelly can wait. It can rot for all I care. I want to talk with you, Lee Ann. I can't hardly function right now. I didn't sleep at all, have barely slept any of the last few days. I have you on my mind constantly. I've never felt what I feel just thinking about you, much less when I'm standing here in front of you and I see the pain in your eyes. I know you're putting on a show for me but I know that something hurts you deep inside." He took another step forward, then reached out and took her hand. It trembled in his so he didn't let go.

His hand was firm and tender at the same time as he led her over to the two rocking chairs that sat on the porch. He couldn't mess this up.

He sat her down in the first one, then he grabbed the other one and pulled it close to hers, their knees touched, and he still held her hand as he leaned forward, his elbows on his knees. He prayed that he didn't mess up.

* * *

Lee Ann was touched by his caring touch and the compassion in his eyes and she couldn't look away.

"Now, Lee Ann, I need to know what happened in your past. *Why?* Why do you not let anybody in that beautiful mind of yours?"

Her heart unleashed in that moment and the truth came out. "I was…a baby, not very old, maybe a few hours old, I don't know. I heard through the grapevine that I was literally laying on the side of the road when I was found. That's why I can't let anyone in. I'm hard. And yet, like I told you before, I don't open my heart to anybody. But this town has caught me, and you, too. I never had anybody look at me the way you look at me. Or hold my hand. Like I told you before, if someone tried to hold my hand. I hurt them, not always, but it was like they were getting in my space. I warned them and they usually drew back."

"I'm glad they didn't hurt you."

"Me too. That's why now I can take care of myself, just in case. But I'm afraid to say this to you, but Max, I like you holding my hand. And looking at me like now, with that caring look in your eyes. But it scares me too. I don't know if I could stay."

Max stayed still. Letting her get out what she needed to say.

Her words rushed out, full of emotion. "There's a chance that if I tried to open my heart to you, you'd be the first person I ever did that with. The first, the one and only. And probably never be anybody else after you. I just…need to let you know the struggle that's going on inside of me right now."

Without saying anything, still holding her hand, he lifted his free hand and cupped her jaw. Oh, the feel of it sent radiation, electric fire burning through her. But the look in his eyes, the tender caring look drilled into her, calming her spirit, taking away the need to run.

"Lee Ann, please give this feeling you feel when we are together a shot. Come with me to the celebration for Norma Sue and Roy Don's anniversary. No strings attached. Just come and enjoy yourself and dance with me."

The feel of his hand, as his fingers brushed the hair from her cheek, sent tingles through her and left her breathless. Then she heard Izzy's grandmas singing in her brain. It was like a dream as her gaze went up toward heaven.

But suddenly, everything changed as she looked up at the sky and the fun song was replaced with *It Is Well With My Soul…it is well…it is well with my soul.*

Her heart tightened and she was overwhelmed as a vision of that poor father stood on that ship and looked out over the water where his children had gone down on their ship. He'd lost his family except for a sweet wife. When that huge ship sank into those deep waters, he'd lost the ones he cared for. Loved… But he stood on the other boat floating on the waters where he'd lost them and he'd sang and the words she'd memorized for some reason radiated though her:

When peace like a river, attendeth my way.

When sorrows like sea billows roll.

Whatever my lot, thou hast taught me to say—

It is well…

It is well…

With my soul…

It is well….It is well with my soul…

Those words haunted her. He'd so loved his family. There was no one in her life who would have ever cared about her enough to sing that song if they'd lost her.

She had never known love like that sweet man had for his family.

No, her family had tossed her. Those who should have cared and loved her had thrown her away. Tossed her to the side of the road and ridden away.

Heart thundering she looked into Max's gaze and felt a deep, deep emotion. Oh, how would it feel to be loved like that? Her eyes teared up and she felt weak.

Weak was something she fought hard not to feel.

Weak was her as a child, not her now in this moment.

"Don't cry," Max said. "I've never tried opening my heart to anyone. And I know you haven't. But I do know it's not weakness." His words slammed into her.

Had he read her mind? "But the thought of letting my guard down is scary. I can't risk falling in love or you falling for me and then me not being able to handle it. Me running away and leaving you tossed to the side of the road. *Then* I would be just like they were. It goes deep, but also, what if you don't care for me the way you think you do."

His hand slipped around to the back of her head. His thumb under her jawline rubbed gently and then he tugged her forehead to his for a moment, before he captured her lips with his.

In that instant, Lee Ann Brown was lost in an array of wonderful emotions that surrounded her, and wiped away all the storms of her soul for that moment.

* * *

The woman had him. He was kissing her, loving her

with all of his heart, and he knew it. If she walked away, he would know exactly how she felt right now. He would know how it felt to be tossed to the side of the road. But he was old enough to know that nobody would ever take her place, no matter what. He loved Lee Ann Brown, loved her more than anything in the world, or there could ever be.

His kiss deepened as his arms went around her. He tugged her from her chair into his lap, and she responded to his kiss. It was like they were one, and in his heart, they were. He closed his eyes and eased up. Heart thundering, he had to get control. This was serious and the one thing he knew, he didn't want to run her off.

"Now he tugged his lips away and she gasped, tears in her eyes. "Max, I'm sorry. I've never felt what I just felt kissing you."

Her words raced through him. "I can promise you, I've never felt what I feel touching you, kissing you, holding you. I love you, Lee Ann Brown. Please don't run away, because I said that. I'm not putting pressure on you. It's just exactly what they said. When it happens, it can come out of nowhere. And you know,

Lee Ann Brown, my bad, Lee Ann Brown. Oh, how I love you. You could take my heart and you can rip it out, and you can chunk it on the side of the road. And I'd still love you. If you need to ride away, you get on your motorcycle and you ride. You do what is best for you, what you need. But you just know that when you go, *my heart* is with you and always will be. *Always.* Nothing will ever take that away. You may ride away but know that there is always a person on this earth who, along with God, loves you, Lee Ann, more than life itself."

Tears appeared. "I just don't know if I can…"

His heart raged with emotion as her eyes showed hope mixed with pain. "Lee Ann, the only thing I love more is Jesus himself. And He's given me a push in the back saying, go, baby. Go."

She was crying, but then she laughed. "Oh my gosh, how can I laugh at a time like this?" She closed her lips. "I can't go crazy right now, but I've never had anybody tell me they love me, *ever*. And it makes me feel happy, scared…and like running. And if what you're saying is true, it's amazing."

He smiled. "I'm not going to put any more pressure on you. I'm going to let you go. We're going to wipe our faces and we're going to finish that prickly pear jelly. And then tomorrow we're not going to do anything. The jelly will all be made and we're going to go to a party. So now I'm asking you formally on a date. Can I take you to the party celebration?"

"Yes." And then she smiled and he…said a prayer.

CHAPTER SEVENTEEN

Lee Ann woke the next morning, Saturday had arrived at last. She sat up in the bed and thought about the day before. Never had she opened her heart like that, but it was the fact that someone loved her.

Max loved her and today she was going on a date to a fifty-year wedding anniversary celebration. She smiled and her gaze landed on her very small group of clothing. What was she going to wear?

She looked at the clock. It was seven. She'd actually slept later than usual so she jumped up, took a shower, washed her hair, pulled it back in a wet, short ponytail, and headed out the door. To her startled surprise, there on a little table beside the door set a plastic container which she could see inside a biscuit and a sausage and a mug of coffee. A note sat beside it. *See you tonight. Five o'clock. Love Max.*

Her heart did a somersault. Oh yeah, her knees went weak again. She knew she was in trouble, but the problem was it didn't really seem like trouble. She picked up breakfast and the note and she headed back outside to the far end of the barn and sat down alone and ate while watching the sun rise higher in the sky, brightening everything up, and peace filled her.

She had a date tonight to get ready for because she had to find something to wear.

She knew it was too early, so she just went for a ride. Her and her motorcycle. She realized that she was riding, that it was the first time she had ever ridden her bike thinking only about the ride and not where or what she was leaving behind.

She smiled at the thought and let the breeze embrace her with the joy it carried through the air.

* * *

"You're taking her to the anniversary party on a date?"

Sam asked as he poured Max a cup of coffee.

Max knew he should have kept his mouth shut, but everybody was going to know it tonight when he and Lee Ann walked into the huge tent that was set up on Clint and Lacy Matlock's ranch. Therefore he might as well try and get some of the craziness out of the way before that happened.

"Does my Adela know?" Sam continued.

"I don't think anybody knows. It's early and Applegate and Stanley are the first guys to know."

The checker players had halted in their game and were looking at him.

Applegate grinned. "You finally asked her out. Good for you."

"It's about time," Stanley said. "You might not have realized it but you never looked at any of them other gals like you do when you look at her."

Sam grinned. "Yup, we've been waitin' for you to get smart."

He grinned, then got serious. "Look, fellas, neither one of us were looking for this. But I like it, and it'll be good for her. But, the truth is she might still get on her motorcycle and ride out of town and never look back. She's got hard things to work through so if you three will pray for her, I'll appreciate it."

They all looked seriously at him and then nodded.

Sam placed his hand on Max's shoulder and gave a squeeze with his powerful grip. "Prayers are going up."

"We've never seen your eyes light up like they do when she's near," Stanley said.

"Have you ridden on the back of her motorcycle?" Applegate asked, bellered was more like it.

"No, I haven't, but maybe I will."

All the old guys laughed.

"What about taking her out there mudding like you always like to do?" Sam asked.

"I want to take her. She would enjoy it." *If she sticks around.* He had high hopes that she would, but nothing guaranteed it. She had a lot in her history to not make her take the chance. Giving her heart away would be rough for her.

It was one thing to let him kiss her and hold her in his arms so she would know how much she meant to him but in the end it was going to come down to if she could do it.

His gaze landed across the street to the ladies' clothing store—it slammed into him that Lee Ann might not have anything to wear to the anniversary party.

He looked at Sam, "What time does Ashby's store open?"

"Nine. Do you need to buy a dress?"

"Not me, but I may need to make sure that Lee Ann has something to wear. I mean, I'll take her in her jeans and her motorcycle boots and the tank top myself, but I think she'll kind of want to blend in. Something tells me she doesn't have dress clothes hidden in that duffle bag that hangs off the side of her motorcycle."

Sam grinned. "Don't go panicking. I know just who to call."

* * *

Lee Ann was just riding around. When she got a call, she could hear her phone ringing because it was connected to her helmet through the sound system. Not that she ever got phone calls, but just in case. So, she slowed her bike and pulled to the side of the road. Who would be calling her?

"Hello? Who's this?" she asked.

"Lacy Brown. I got your number from Pollyanna since you gave it to her when you checked in the other day."

"Yes, I never get calls, so why did you need it?"

"We heard you have a date tonight and we want to meet you at Ashby's and help you pick out something to wear. All the ladies want to get you dressed up for the party."

Everybody knew she had a date and they were going to dress her up. "Lacy, I never dressed up before."

Lacy chuckled. "Well, come to town, girlfriend. We're going to have the time of our life helping you find the right outfit for the evening. Believe me, there's going to be a crowd. The word is passed around and everybody's as excited about getting you dressed for this date as they are about the anniversary party. Heck, it's Norma Sue's party and she's overjoyed to see you having a date."

"Really—"

"We just know you've never done this and well, Max doesn't date either and he's special to every one of us since we watched him from the day he came to town on the van. So, we're excited to see him bringing you to the dance. No pressure. So, come to Ashby's store. We're going to be waiting and I can't tell you who, but it's all paid for so don't worry about that. And you're making someone's day by letting them do this."

Lee Ann stared across the surrounding pastures letting the call sink in. Then she smiled and headed toward Mule Hollow. She was going to get dressed up. She smiled as the wind blew in her face. It didn't take long, and she rolled into Mule Hollow. She knew exactly where the store was, just right down the street within sight of Sam's.

And in front of Sam's was Max's truck. Her heart rampaged again. Literally, she parked her bike in one of the few slots open. There was a big old truck that she knew Norma Sue drove, and there was Esther Mae's Volkswagen, Lacy's pink Caddy, and Izzy's Thunderbird sitting right in front of the store. It seemed everybody had gotten a call. Her heart was thundering at the thought of all these people wanting to help her hit hard.

Hit her heart. She closed her eyes. "Thank You." And then she forced herself not to throw a look back toward the diner. She knew she was being watched from there too, because she knew Sam, Applegate, and Stanley were probably looking out that front window. And since his truck was there, Max too.

She'd just stepped onto the plank sidewalk when the clothing store door flew open and Esther Mae rushed out. "I'm so glad we got the call. We're so excited. Now. Come on in here. Everybody's waiting. Let's get this fun party started."

* * *

She was beautiful. Max stood in the barn, stunned, not because he hadn't expected her to look amazing, but just stunned by everything running through him seeing Lee Ann Brown dressed up. She looked as feminine and sweet as could be. She wore a pastel flowing dress that hung right above her knees, so her knees and her calves and her ankles and her feet all showed. And she even wore a pair of high heels.

This tough cookie didn't look tough right now. She looked, "Amazing." The word came out in a gush.

Her eyes glowed and then she laughed, and he did too, seeing her joy.

"I love it," she said. "Honestly, I never even thought about dressing up before. So anyway, it's going to be fun and that's what I'm going to think about tonight. Just relaxing and having fun with you and everybody in Mule Hollow."

He grinned and held out his elbow. "Then slip your arm through mine and let's head to my truck and on to the party. And I hope some dancing."

She slipped her arm through his, their gazes met and he smiled then she smiled, and then they headed to his truck.

Had to make sure he didn't do anything to scare her or put too much pressure on her. His mom and his dad had realized the moment he had walked into their house after breakfast that something was going on. He hadn't told them everything, but he told him he had a date. And they had been amazed because he wasn't a dater.

His mom looked up at his dad, who put his arm around her shoulders. "Your mom and I made a mistake early on but you came from that mistake and so we don't regret it. Nothing in our life would ever be right if you weren't with us. So, we're rooting for you to go have a good time tonight. And just know we love you and we're behind you and hope to meet this wonderful lady whose gotten your attention."

He'd grinned. "Say a prayer for her. She has a lot going on in her heart and needs all the prayers to help her adjust to everything that's happening in her life."

His mom had come over and hugged him. "We are praying."

That was his parents. They were happy for him and he knew they would be praying for Lee Ann. And also that he and Lee Ann would have a good time.

And now as he helped Lee Ann get into his truck, he was already having a great time. He held the truck door open and she scooted into the seat. Then he reached over and grabbed the seatbelt, pulled it around her. "We're going to have a good time. No strain or worrying allowed. Tonight is tonight."

She met his gaze and gave a gentle smile. "Exactly."

* * *

Everyone went through the line congratulating Norma Sue and Roy Don on their anniversary. The robust couple both grinned widely as Lee Ann and Max made it to them.

"Congratulations," he said as Norma Sue grabbed him around the waist and hugged him.

"Thank you." She beamed up at him with that wide smile of hers. "I'm a blessed woman with my Roy Don. We plan to make the next fifty years the best years of our marriage. We're so glad you two came to help us celebrate." She reached out one arm and pulled Lee Ann into the hug. Roy Don watched, grinning. "Glad you haven't hopped on your motorcycle yet. You two enjoy yourselves."

Lee Ann was smiling and Max's heart swelled with the love he felt for her. Loved that she was literally being embarrassed by the town as everyone was watching and smiling.

"I already am," she told Norma Sue, who then released them. "Great, that makes our celebration perfect."

Then they were pushed forward as the next well-wishers stepped up to celebrate with the couple. He and Lee Ann went to the table where several of his friends, including Jake and Cassie, were right there waiting.

"Y'all are looking good all dressed up," Cassie said.

Jake agreed. "Y'all need to go mudding with us next weekend."

"Yes, y'all need to. Lee Ann, you want to do that, don't you?"

"You have me curious about it."

Her answer gave him hope that she would still be around.

And then the dancing began. He watched Norma Sue and Roy Don lead the way out onto the dance floor to dance to the first song, and then everybody was out there. He stood up and held his hand out, and Lee Ann slipped her hand in his and he led her out to the dance floor.

She had pre-warned him that she couldn't dance, and he'd assured her that he would lead the way. And he did as they danced slowly. She followed the steps, but he wasn't thinking about any of that. She fit in his arms just right, they were in sync, and she was meant to be in his arms. He pushed all his worries about her leaving tomorrow away and just enjoyed holding her and making sure that Lee Ann Brown had a good time. Holding her in his arms made his night the best it had ever been.

CHAPTER EIGHTEEN

ee Ann loved dancing with Max, being held by him as they danced. It was an amazing night. Esther Mae, sweet, flamboyant Esther May in her colorful dress that had a full skirt that looked like a swirling rainbow that matched the huge smile that radiated from her heart.

"I'm so glad you two are here," she said, giving them a thumbs up as Hank twirled her around and on past them.

Sweet Esther Mae. That woman, well, all of them connected with Lee Ann and she felt like she was among family. Max squeezed her close as if he heard her thoughts. She looked at him and knew this was a night she'd never forget.

Finally, it was over and she went and gave the ladies hugs and thanked each one of them for helping her pick out the dress that helped her have the time of her life, and it really had been the best time she'd ever had.

Then she and Max headed back to the truck. "It felt like I was in a dream," she said as he opened the truck door. She stepped into the section between the door, the truck and him. Instead of getting in the seat she turned toward him. "I had a wonderful time."

"Yes, it was," he said, cupping her face with his hands, he dipped his head and kissed her. "One I'll never forget."

Heart racing, she nodded, soaking up all the feelings that were surrounding her. She turned and got into the truck. She grabbed the seatbelt before Max had time to reach for it.

Silence surrounded them as they drove away. It was as if they both knew the night was coming to an end. Her thoughts shifted to how open she'd made her heart tonight. How exposed she now was to pain if something were to happen, she was no longer in control.

They just pulled into the drive and she looked over at him. "You know, you said your mom got pregnant when she was in protective custody because she and your dad went out of bounds. They let emotions take over and they made a mistake, but they're grateful. After all, they got you out of it."

"Yes I remember," he said, his voice gentle.

"I wonder if my mom ever looks back and wishes she hadn't tossed me out the car."

Max didn't say anything. Instead he got out of the truck, strode around the truck and opened her door. She'd already unbuckled her seatbelt, but she couldn't move. He stepped into the area between the door and her and put one elbow on the top of the window and leaned in with his other hand cupped on her cheek. Oh, how she loved his gentle touch.

"Lee Ann, knowing what your mother was thinking is something we will never know. But I can tell you that sometimes people make mistakes and they live to regret them, and I'm going to say that your dad, like my dad, might've never known that you existed. Who knows with research, we may be able to find him."

"I thought about that a long time ago, but that's where I can't go. You know me. I do what I do, and I won't crawl. To me, that door is shut. But sometimes I still wonder if my mother ever regrets what she did?"

His thumb paused from stroking her cheek, moved under her chin and lifted it so that her eyes and his were straight on. "I can tell you this, Lee Ann, God has a plan for you. He gave you strength and an attitude and a *fighting* spirit. *He* made you into the wonderful woman that you are. The woman I love. I'm sorry but tonight showed me that I want a life with you in it. I have to say, as horrible as it is to say, if what happened to you hadn't happened, you might not be the person you are today. You wouldn't have been riding that motorcycle into my prickly pears and had a flat at just the right moment for us to meet. You have overcome huge sadness and become a wonderful woman. God has a plan."

She couldn't speak, her heart twisted with the pain that was fighting the happiness she'd felt tonight. The touch of this man and the heart of this man had her world spinning but it wasn't making things easier…

It was making things harder.

"Again, you're going to do what you need to do, but whatever you do, you're going to know that I love you." He gently pulled her from the truck, embraced her, and then he kissed her, long, deep, heartfelt. His kiss reached to her toes and lifted her up off the ground. Her arms went around him and she squeezed hard because in her heart of hearts, now she was thinking of Pollyanna having lost her first husband that she loved. Yes, she'd found love again but the pain of loss…did she want to live it as an adult?

She'd spent her life keeping her heart free, so now, knowing how much she loved Max now, could she give everything to him and let that love grow and then lose it?

Heart thundering, she kissed Max with everything in her heart and soul, but in her mind she couldn't give everything. She had to keep control so she pulled away and as their lips parted she tried not to cry.

The moonlight shone around them. "I love you, Lee Ann Brown. I am always going to be here for you." And then he let her go, then he simply walked away.

She stood there in the moonlight watching him,

knowing that he was not pressuring her and was going to take whatever she came up with. She turned and headed down the hall of the barn and didn't stop until she got to the end and sank down on the box. She pulled her knees up and wrapped her arms around them as she lay her forehead on her knees and she cried.

* * *

Max didn't have a good feeling as he had walked away. He felt her arms as she'd kissed him. It was as if she was saying goodbye.

It was a kiss that knocked his knees out from underneath him, and it was everything he could do to stay standing. He wasn't going to ask her to stay. He'd said from the beginning it was her choice. But he would love her always. He was strong.

He made it to his house and inside with the door closed behind him, and he sank into the first chair he reached. He'd sat there for a long, long time and he prayed. This wasn't all about him. It was about Lee Ann and it would be whatever she made it.

Later he'd gone to bed and hadn't slept much. But now, Sunday morning, he was in the kitchen, making coffee, forcing himself to take his time. Finally, coffee in hand he walked outside hoping she was already waiting for him to bring her a cup. But her motorcycle was gone.

He stopped on the porch and sank down to sit on the top step. Lee Ann Brown was gone. It hit him. Lacy Brown had stayed in town. Lee Ann Brown had ridden away. He forced himself to get up. He'd known this could happen.

He forced himself inside and he dressed for church. He had told her he wouldn't let it kill him or tear him up. He'd just pray that she got everything she needed and God blessed her. And then he strode outside and got in his truck and he headed to church.

Cars were everywhere. This little church was beautiful. It sat there forever, and the crowd had grown, and Chance, the preacher, had been a rodeo preacher who was always strong and spoke blunt words of God. Today Max needed a sermon that helped him deal with the trauma going on inside of him.

He pulled his shoulders back, determined that he would be strong, as he strode across the grass toward the church doors. He could handle this. He realized that people saw him coming alone. His expression was tense and his eyes were on the doors that he was headed for. They parted and let him pass, nobody really said anything. He couldn't talk. He just knew the Lord would give him strength. He walked inside, walked up and sat down in the aisle seat in the front of the church, because he wanted as few people as possible seeing the expression of pain he knew was on his face.

Behind him he heard the church filling up. The choir came in and filled up their seats in front then Pastor Chance walked in. "Welcome," he said, his gaze rested for a moment on Max.

Max nodded then looked down at his hands that were clasped in his lap.

Thankfully, everybody obviously could tell he was dealing with something deep and left him alone. Then as the music started Jake and Cassie came and sat down beside him. Cassie in the middle, not too close but she patted his knee and then she took her husband's hand,

and Max knew they were praying for him.

But they were giving him his space. Sometimes people just needed space. Maybe he should have gone to the river and just sat alone. Maybe he shouldn't have come to church but instead closed himself up in the house and not taken this chance of coming out here so everybody could see his pain.

But he was here and he could do this.

He had told Lee Ann to do what she needed to do and he'd meant it.

Pastor Chance had been welcoming everyone and now everybody was standing up as Adela had started playing the piano. The singing started.

Max forced himself to stand, but he didn't sing. He just listened to the three songs they sang.

Then they sat down and Lilly, tiny Lilly Tipps Wells with the amazing voice, stood alone for the special solo. The music started and she softly began singing—his heart clenched as her first words were words he needed to hear—*Be Still and Know That I Am God*. Tears welled in his eyes and he fought them down as Lilly continued.

He knew God, and he knew God knew he needed to give this to Him.

Max's heart ached, thundered as the song reached deep.

The words of that song and the soft, lyrical voice of Lilly helped calm him. He'd done what he needed to do by keeping the pressure off the woman he loved.

Be Still And Know That I Am God…he knew.

He looked up and saw that Lilly was looking straight at him, knowing the words were for him and she sent him a gentle smile as the lyrics repeated. Then her gaze shifted and her eyes twinkled as she sang again. He heard a slight commotion in the back of the church but he was focused on the song as the church went silent.

Be Still and Know That I Am God…he felt a soft touch to his shoulder. A gentle touch and he looked up straight into the tear-filled eyes of Lee Ann.

The whole church went silent. "I rode away but as far as I rode trying to get away from the possible pain loving you would bring. I stopped at the top of a hill and listened to the soft song that has played inside of me for years. The song that I could never relate too. But I gave in and I came back to you. And God, He is so sneaky and wonderful because I walked inside and Lilly is singing the song that I finally did. I was still on the top of that hill and I listened. Max, I know now that God led me here and He gave me you."

Max's heart rammed into his ribs and he stood.

"I just had to be still and know that in you, He's given me your love, full of everything my heart needs. You and your love of God and me is everything I need."

He stood up, tears rolled down his face, yes, he was crying as he swept Lee Ann into his arms, buried his head against her neck, and everything in his world clicked into place. The entire church filled with cheers as he spun in the aisle with the love of his life embraced in his arms.

And then he halted, lifted his head and he looked at her. "Lee Ann Brown, I love you and I want you to be my wife."

Her beautiful smile blasted across her face. "Yes, I get two wonderful things with that yes. I get you and I will no longer be bad, bad Lee Ann Brown, I'll be Lee Ann Cantrell, the happiest woman around. Whether we have five minutes, five years or a hundred years, I will love you for as long as God gives us."

He was grinning. "Oh what a life we're going to have." He couldn't help it he kissed her again.

Pastor Chance walked up and placed a hand on each of their shoulders. "God gives us happy endings every day in His own wonderful way."

"Yes He does," Max agreed knowing it was so very true.

"Now, Lee Ann, you can take that man of yours on a ride on that motorcycle of yours," Esther Mae called.

Everybody started clapping and laughing. Lee Ann was glowing, not crying anymore but smiling. "She's right, cowboy. How about we go get on my motorcycle right now and go for a ride of a lifetime?"

"I'll ride anywhere with you." Hand in hand, they walked out of the church with everybody cheering and then, smiling he climbed on the back of that motorcycle and let his soon-to-be bride drive. She slipped onto the seat in front of him, handed him her red helmet. "Put this on."

"No, you put it on."

"Wait," yelled Esther Mae as she ran past them to her car then spun and came back holding her sparkling helmet that she handed to Lee Ann. "Here you go, sweet, sweet Lee Ann Brown. Take that man for the ride of a lifetime."

He loved his life. Lee Ann took the helmet and pulled it onto her head as he did the same, and then she turned and kissed him quickly. "Now hold on, cowboy, and let's ride."

Oh what a great life it was going to be. He wrapped his arms around her, leaned in close and let his Lee Ann gun the engine and then they rode.

This was going to be the ride of a lifetime and he was so glad that his bad, bad Lee Ann Brown had come to town and won his heart.

A smile spread across his face. "I'll always be thankful you listened and came back."

"Me too." She slowed the motorcycle on the hilltop overlooking Mule Hollow. Then she brought it to a halt, placed her booted feet on the ground, turned her body so that her shoulder was touching his heart as she leaned into him and planted a kiss on his waiting lips.

Love…oh what a blessing it was.

About the Author

Debra Clopton is a USA Today bestselling & International bestselling author who has sold over 3.5 million books. She has published over 81 books under her name and her pen name of Hope Moore.

Under both names she writes clean & wholesome and inspirational, small town romances, especially with cowboys but also loves to sweep readers away with romances set on beautiful beaches surrounded by topaz water and romantic sunsets.

Her books now sell worldwide and are regulars on the Bestseller list in the United States and around the world. Debra is a multiple award-winning author, but of all her awards, it is her reader's praise she values most. If she can make someone smile and forget their worries for a few hours (or days when binge reading one of her series) then she's done her job and her heart is happy. She really loves hearing she kept a reader from doing the dishes or sleeping!

A sixth-generation Texan, Debra lives on a ranch in Texas with her husband surrounded by cattle, deer, very busy squirrels and hole digging wild hogs. She enjoys traveling and spending time with her family.

Visit Debra's website and sign up for her newsletter for updates at: www.debraclopton.com

Check out her Facebook at: www.facebook.com/debra.clopton.5

Follow her on Instagram at: debraclopton_author

or contact her at debraclopton@ymail.com

www.ingramcontent.com/pod-product-compliance
Lightning Source LLC
Chambersburg PA
CBHW070636100726
47907CB00007B/2006